To Shau
Hope ya

C000036931

First ever signed copy
of this book!

TOWN

www.stephenmosley.net

ISBN: 979-8-4572-6085-6

CONTENTS

1. THE TOWN

Trapped beneath a domed, ashen sky, the town was sliced in two by a meandering river and surrounded by woodland. An old dirt road provided the only exit, but rumour maintained that it went on forever. No one ever dared to find out.

Everyone knew everyone here, but would rather they didn't. One could not shed a solitary tear within their own private confines without Mr Reed, down the road, knowing you were weak. Or Joyce Burke, on the other side of town, feeling thankful that her own tears were comfortably repressed.

Every weekend, the people engaged in hearsay over a pint of weak bitter at the Fox & Newt pub, by the river. This pint was synonymous with bringing these people together, but only if there was gossip to be had. And for those who made up what they didn't know, there would always be plenty of that: Spilling from lips as muffled vulgarities; causing humiliation to whomever happened to be absent. Aside from this once or twice-weekly event, conversation was left on the sidelines. And this is the way they liked it.

Outsiders to the town would joke that its residents were inter-bred—an unknowing joke as it may contain some element of truth: No one here really knew where they came from; history was missing from their minds, as was the future.

When one town-dweller boldly remarked that he lived for the moment, he was merely hiding the painful awareness that he had no future.

As for the present, that was a haze: It always felt like seven a.m. on a Monday morning, when the people awoke to the routine humdrum of their ordinary lives, kicking and screaming from the comfort of dreams.

Mr Reed danced through Dreamland with the athletic grace of Gene Kelly—but when he awoke, and left the house to go to work, the only thing dancing was the rain on his face.

Joyce Burke was transformed by sleep into the woman she wanted to be: A splendiferous being, who commanded respect and earned affection.

When she awoke, though, she lamented her lack of control over the 13 unruly children she gave special classes to at the local school—a realisation that greeted her, as sure as the rain, every morning.

Yet she knew, in her heart, that one mustn't grumble. Not when there was work to be done. And there would always be plenty of that: Grime cleansed from dishes, creases ironed from shirts, dust flurrying from every surface. She wished everything else could be cleansed, ironed and dusted away with the same dismissive ease.

Joyce could be safe, for a moment, within her dreams; but others were not so lucky.

In a house atop the wooded hills, 19-year-old Beth Anderson was getting ready to go out. Darkening her eyes, smearing her lips, squeezing into clothes she wouldn't usually wear; she promised her folks she wouldn't be too late back, before stepping out into a cold dark Thursday.

In the town centre, Darren Thompson closed the doors of his father's garage, Thompson Motors. Wiping the grease from his hands, he sent his best mate and co-worker, Benny, home, and waited for Beth to arrive.

Over the road at Tony's Grotto, one-eyed music-shop owner, Tony, placed another record on the turntable with pudgy hands.

And in the tenement block, on the outskirts of town, there lived a boy named Marvin Jeffreys— better known as Marv—whose eyes stayed open when others' were closed.

You'd be forgiven for thinking that all it does here is rain, but sometimes things happened.

2. MARV

Marv had artistic leanings. In this town, that was as bad as having dandruff.

Someday the world would notice him. He would be adored throughout for his poetry. After all, he'd read worse. Until then, all he needed to do was get some rest, get some sleep—find peace of mind for once in his life. After that, the world was his oyster. And like an oyster, it would probably be grey, squishy and horrible. He hated the way he thought sometimes. His mind had a mind of its own.

All the people in this town
Live with their heads against the ground.
They never dare look beyond the sky,
They haven't begun to question the reason why.

When I say love, they think of rape,
When I hold out my hand, they want to fight.
It's no wonder I'm in nervous shape
When people like that dwell outside.

Every soul in this town grows up mistaking
Life for death, and giving for taking.
Why, oh why must all beauty be stolen,
Whilst ignorance and hatred are overly swollen.

And why won't my God send this Beast his Beauty,
Or at least send an angel with a gun just to shoot me,
To release me from this mire that I sink in,

And the thoughts in my brain that I w
thinking.

Only in rare dreams can I almost just feel
Any love I may need in this world they call real.

Marv stopped writing and closed his notebook. He hadn't moved from his bed in hours. His eyes stung as if embedded in hot gravels. He'd been waiting too long in this creased position for sleep's unpunctual embrace. Beneath his sweating legs, the mattress had assumed a texture like rotting, leprous flesh; blankets yellowed like ancient tomes, sporting dark stains like bruises on fruit.

The mattress sat on the floor of a small, cluttered room. Books, DVDs and vinyl records spiralled towards the low, cracked ceiling in uneven, swaying towers. At the foot of the bed, like a portal in the dark, was an old TV with colours tuned too high. Every image that stained its screen seemed garish and unreal. But night was less lonely by the light of its glow.

Without getting up, Marv plucked a book from a nearby pile. But his brain wouldn't focus; the words all blurred on the page. He tossed the book away and scratched his greasy, black hair. Despite being only 18, he felt as though a little, hunchbacked man had taken residence in his heart. And, curled there like a melancholy dog, this misshapen sprite roared out its thoughts:

I could quite happily be buried here, in this tomb-like room—like a Mummy, surrounded in death by the possessions it loved in life . . .

As Thursday night rolled on, he continued to sit, propped up on flat pillows; a broken doll in stained underwear and a T-shirt bearing the skull-like visage of Morbius Mozella.

Mozella was Marv's favourite actor. He had played the Mummy. In fact, he had played *all* the great roles: the Vampire, the Werewolf, the Frankenstein Creature . . . Marv liked monsters. He knew how they felt. And he saw them everywhere.

They blinked at him from the shadows, oozing across the room. They lived inside his skull, and chattered in his ears:

Why can't I be like everybody else?

Thankfully, Marv did see beauty. Just not where others saw it. He found it in the late-night movies that swam inside his TV. He saw it in the trashy paperbacks he read from cover to cover. And he heard it in the old recordings he cherished more than life.

Movies they never saw, books they never read, and records they'd never heard of. That was his life.

Flipping through his notebook, he found the sellotaped news clipping. *ANOTHER RIVER SUICIDE* shrieked the headline. He stared at the torn photo of the dead woman. Her name was Victoria Jeffreys. She'd been found in the river two years ago. She was his mother.

He'd never known his father; he'd left when Marv was a baby, but his mother had been special. From her, Marv inherited his love of old books, music and art. And now he was left all alone in the flat they once shared, writing his poems of love and injustice.

How could life end so cruelly? Why do babies get cancer? Why are children run down?

His mind continued to wander.

He wished he could switch himself off like a machine.

I hope all this misery will propel me to do something great someday. He knew more than he cared about the eighth day Someday—the day that never comes.

Until then, Marv battled Insomnia, a creature that had plagued him all his life. He personified it in his mind as a slimy, toad-like monster with flesh like burnt cheese. (Marv was allergic to cheese. It made his stomach swell.)

Bereft of ray gun, or any kind of weapon, he battled the alien fiend alone, wrestling it with spindly arms on a barren landscape. He became a hero: Marvellous Marvo—a character created in infancy, a fabulous alter ego.

When the monster was defeated, he would enter Dreamland—the only place where he could see his mum again.

3. BETH & DARREN

With her raven bangs and light-green eyes, Beth had always been told she looked like a pixie; that she ought to be haunting enchanted forests, or sidling beneath magic toadstools. But she wasn't. She was lying on her back, on the dirty concrete floor of Thompson Motors, with her knickers round her knees, and her boyfriend's shaven head huffing above her. She'd almost forgotten he was there, until he suddenly stopped. "Are you all right?" she asked.

Darren sniffed. "Yeah. 'Course I am."

Beth detected a silence that needed filling. "I mean, it's all right if you're not—"

"Of course I'm all right," Darren snapped. "What's wrong with you?"

"Nothing—"

"Well, shut the fuck up, then."

Beth rose on one elbow. "You don't have to talk to me like that." She wished he would shave off his bum-fluff moustache. "I only wanted to know if you were all right."

"Fine," Darren grunted. Then he pushed her down and started thrusting again.

"Wait."

Darren stopped. "What is it now?"

"You're not all right, are you?"

Jumping to his feet, he pulled up his jeans.

Beth dragged her knickers back over her thighs. "Why are you being like this?"

"I said I was fine." Fumbling in the dark for his shirt, he found it draped over a spare tyre. Then he started looking for his socks.

"You can tell me anything, you know? I'm your girlfriend."

Darren put his shirt on. He still hadn't found his socks. "It's late," he said. "Why don't you go home?"

She got up and touched his shoulder. He felt like cold stone.

"Just go," he said.

She found her parka lying over a bonnet. Putting it on, she walked to the garage doors then turned. Slumped in the shadows, surrounded by wrecked cars, her boyfriend looked a pitiful sight.

"Darren?" she whispered.

He lifted his head.

"Here's your fucking socks." She flung them in his face and stepped out.

The streets were long, wet and empty. Wind rushed past the vacant shops and around the towering war monument. Beth zipped up her parka. It was starting to rain.

Oh great, and I'm in this stupid skirt.

She hated short skirts; she had only worn it for him. Looking over her shoulder at the garage, she waited for Darren to run out, take her in his arms and tell her he was sorry. But he didn't.

So, she kept on walking: past the chemist's, the butcher's and Tony's Grotto. A bloated shadow danced across the upstairs window of the music shop. At first, she thought it was a ghost. But when the shadow passed again, she saw that it was only Tony.

Strange man.

It was a perfect night for seeing ghosts. An old car humped its way down the road, slowing to a stop beside her. Beth's heart flinched.

The window rolled down, and a ruddy face poked through.

"Are you all right, my dear?"

It was only Mr Reed. His wife was sitting beside him in the passenger seat.

Phew.

"Yes. I'm fine, thank you."

"You're sure? You look . . ."

"I'm fine."

Christ, why is it so normal to lie?

Reed smiled at her. Not only were there lipstick smears around his lips, but his shirt was untucked, his tie was loose, and he stank of beer. "Tickle your arse with a feather," he leered.

"What?"

He looked alarmed, then pointed to the drizzling skies. "I said 'typical nasty weather'."

"Oh. Yeah." *Maybe he did.* "Good night." She walked on, trainers squelching on damp stone.

"Do you have a nice pussy, Miss Anderson?"

She froze. *Why is he asking me that? In front of his wife?* Beth turned slowly. "What?"

Reed was grinning through the rolled-down window. "A *cat*, Miss Anderson. Do you have a cat?"

Beth wrinkled her nose. "No. Why?"

"Oh, nothing. Just wondered. Good night."

Weirdo.

She walked away, quicker this time.

"If you must know," he called out behind her: "I wanted to warn you. They're filthy creatures. Never trust a cat."

"Good night, Mr Reed," she said, keeping forward. He was probably drunk.

As she turned the corner, she waited for Reed's engine to start. But it didn't. Peering back, she noticed he was still parked crooked at the kerb.

He was watching her through the car window. She could feel his eyes rolling like iced jellies across her skin.

It's all right, she told herself, *he's not going to rape me; he's with his wife.* She could see her shadow in the passenger seat. *He just wants to see that I'm all right. He's concerned about me, that's all.* People were always thinking the worst of each other. Especially in this town. And Mr Reed was a good man. Everyone knew that. Having managed the old people's home for so long, he was now a full-time carer for his disabled wife.

Beth watched the couple exchange a loving glance, before snuggling together. It looked like they were settling down for a nap. And why not? It was long after midnight.

But why are they out so late?

She saw Mr Reed again, in her mind's eye, watching her from his window: eyes goggling, mouth frothing, furred tongue licking the glass. *Do you have a nice pussy, Miss Anderson?* She shook the image from her brain.

They must have just left the pub. They've had one too many. That's all. They're just sleeping it off. It wouldn't be right to drink and drive. In silhouette, they looked just like two teenagers in love. Like Darren and herself.

She moved on through the rain, passing the cemetery gates. From beyond their iron curls, she heard whispers in the dark. She started to run.

Down winding cobbles, through filthy alleys, she raced up the hill to her parents' house. Letting herself in, she wrapped a towel round her head and trudged upstairs. Safe within her room, she flicked on the stereo and flopped into bed to the strains of her favourite singer, Jonas Koop.

Sweet Beth Anderson, all of 19. She should have been haunting an enchanted forest, or sidling beneath magic toadstools. But, as it was, she lay crumpled in her bedroom, crying in the dark.

4. DREAMLAND

Marv had entered Dreamland. In the endless dark behind his eyes, a figure stepped towards him. It was his mother, shimmering in a white shroud. She was trying to tell him something, but he couldn't quite hear. He felt himself drifting closer, until his hand was gripped by hers. The fingers were cold and fragile, as if her bones were spun from glass.

Close-up, he saw a gaping, bloody hole in her chest. The blood ran down to her thighs, staining her shroud. He looked to her face. Her eyes stood out, vast as green oceans, filling with sadness and hurt. Her mouth was an immovable slit. He wished he could make her smile again.

A pale grey fog swirled around them and Victoria was lost to the mists once more. A loud noise filled Marv's ears; the sound of an orchestra falling to pieces. The mists parted with a hiss.

And then, a smell: familiar and septic; like boiled cabbage and hospital corridors . . .

He knew where he was. At school again.

He stood in the dingy classroom, shirt hanging out of his trousers, tie hanging loose round his neck. He felt last year's acne burning on his skin. He hated being a teenager.

The rest of the class surrounded him, laughing and pointing, their faces distorted.

Darren Thompson came forwards, holding out a block of cheese.

"Here you are, Starving Marvin: I've got some food for you!"

They know I'm allergic to cheese.

Darren chased Marv round the classroom. "Eat the cheese, bitch!"

Everyone laughed as Marv scrabbled and stumbled over tables and chairs, trying to get away. He banged against cupboards and doors. Then, tripping over his undone laces, he slammed to the floor. And something hard and smelly struck his lips.

Darren was standing over him, teeth clenched, thrusting the cheese into Marv's mouth.

Ha-ha-ha-ha-ha-ha.

Everyone hooted as Marv swallowed the offending fromage. "No!" he retched. "My allergy . . ."

But it was too late. His stomach rumbled, swelling like a balloon. Stretching, growing . . . finally, it burst. Entrails hit their faces. Blood splattered the walls. Yet still they continued to laugh.

Marv's vision began to fade. The last person he saw was his friend Beth Anderson. She was the only one with a straight face; the only one not covered in his guts.

A mist descended. When it parted, he was whole again and gazing from the window of another classroom. Beth was outside, standing alone by the school gates.

Marv needed to talk to her; to ask her why she no longer sat with him at the back of class, drawing cartoons, making up stories, singing old songs.

"Eyes to the front, bozo."

It was the biology teacher, Mr 'Cranky' Shankly, who sat behind his desk, looking severe. Before him, a roomful of hunched students scribbled on exam papers. Marv inspected the blank piece of paper on his desk. He hadn't revised and the questions made no sense.

He looked again to the window. Beth was still standing at the gates. He *had* to rush out and see her.

"I said, eyes to the front."

Marv hated school. He tried to write an answer, but his mind was as blank as the page. Despite his warning from old 'Cranky', he gave the window another glance. Beth was still there. But she was no longer alone. She was pressed against the gates, kissing Darren.

Marv's heart shattered on the spot.

He'd never seen them exchange two words before, and here they were exchanging spittle. He watched them walk away, arm in arm.

This isn't the way it's supposed to be.

The mists again made their entrance, and Marv felt himself drifting through time. When the fog cleared, he was standing outside the local hotel, clutching an old book he'd inherited from his mother.

It was the night of the end-of-school dance. He remembered it well—unfortunately.

Putting his book down, he pulled himself up to the window and saw all his classmates, looking half-glamorous in fancy frocks that would never be worn again. Laughing and dancing, they seemed to be bathed in a golden light. How did it all come so easily to them?

He saw Beth. How he wished he was in there with her. Whilst lost in her beauty, a glass bottle exploded against the wall right next to his head. Slipping down to the gravel, he heard shoes crunch their way towards him. It was Darren and his best mate, Benny. They'd been sneaking gulps of booze in a nearby bush.

"Looks like we've got a peeping tom," said Darren, yanking Marv to his feet. "Fucking perv."

Benny picked up Marv's book and stared at the blank cover. "What the fuck is this shit?" He tossed it into the shrubbery. "Fucking weird shit. Fucking weirdo."

"That was my mother's," Marv protested.

"Well, she ain't gonna read it," said Darren. "She's dead."

Laughing, the boys circled their prey, singing "Your mummy's dead" to the tune of "Auld Lang Syne".

Marv covered his ears, but Darren shoved him back against a hedge—then kept on pushing.

Marv found himself lost in a maze of twigs; scraping his flesh; tearing his clothes. The hedge grew vast around him, engulfing him in its twisted thickets.

And on the other side was the graveyard, where his mother lay, devoured by worms.

Marv unleashed a piercing scream.

Then he awoke into a silence that seemed even louder.

5. JOYCE & ARTHUR

Friday morning slammed against the windows, but was kept at bay by plain white net curtains.

Joyce Burke wasn't needed at the school until after lunch. Time had to be killed somehow, so a spot of retail therapy seemed the perfect execution. She had run out of gin.

For Joyce, love was still packaged in bottles at the local off-licence. She hated the taste, but loved the promise of its glow. The town's water was undrinkable (it was known to rot your teeth).

Dreams made her pretty and drink made her smart. Sometimes, when drunk, she could rule the world, starting from tomorrow. But tomorrow was a fiction; a day that never came.

Work was not going well. She was having particular problems with Wayne, the boy who had been thrown out of a window by his dad. Joyce had been trying to teach Wayne how to count to 10 in French.

"Une, deux, TWAT!" he kept saying with glee.

"*Trois*, Wayne, *trois*." Joyce seemed to spend her whole life trying to regain dignity. "Let's try again."

"Une, deux, *TWAT!*"

And so it went on.

Still, at least the weekend was almost here. But Saturdays were hungover, and Sundays brought worries. And, before you knew it, it was Monday again.

Her husband, Arthur, had retired from the post office. Now he had all the time in the world to play with his toys. They weren't toys to him, though. His trains were his pride and joy.

Arthur had built a whole world in his attic: Lines of gleaming tracks; tiny plastic trees, little plastic people; all at the control of an electric box. He even had stereo systems wired up, booming out ambience: the enthusiastic sounds of gleeful children and friendly adults. A world he'd once known, now lost, trapped as sounds in an old man's attic. Notebooks full of numbers; happy days whiled away on platforms, feeling young.

He loved trains. They made him a child again, kept adulthood at bay. Bills, arthritis and chest pains were forgotten. As was the wife.

No.

He loved his wife. He just loved trains more.

He stood amidst the tracks, flicking switches; his watery eyes glowing like those of a doting father as the trains clacked around him. An old engine driver's cap was perched atop his head at a jaunty angle. Sometimes he made hooting noises: "*Whoo-whooooo!*"

His wife emerged through the attic trap, her face drooping with disgust. "Playing with your toys again?"

"Hello, darling. I didn't see you there."

"I'm off into town before work. Is there anything you want from the shops?"

But Arthur was transfixed by the noise of his trains. *Clickety-clack. Clickety-clack.* "Oh, nothing special, darling," he said, after a while. "Whatever you want is fine with me."

"It'll have to be fish fingers, then. Those steak pies were very disappointing."

Arthur wasn't listening.

"You love them more than me, don't you?" she said.

"Sorry?" he squinted. "Fish fingers?"

"You heard."

As she bobbed back down the ladder, Arthur made a hooting noise above. *"Whooo-whooooo!"*

In her mind's eye, Joyce could see his dry, pursed lips and stupid cap. She hoisted herself back up, jabbing her face through the trap. "I said: you love them more than me, don't you?"

Arthur grew still. "I love you, darling. You know that."

"You love trains more," said Joyce. "You even love them more than Olivia."

Arthur looked at her for the first time that day. Then he looked at his shoes.

He was still looking at them when his wife descended the ladder and thudded her way downstairs. He heard the clinking of bottles in the kitchen, the rustled gathering of coat and bag. And then the front door made a noise like a small explosion.

Arthur removed his train driver's cap and scrunched it in his hands. Then, trembling, he sank to the floor.

6. LOVE, DEATH & ROCK 'N' ROLL

As soon as Marv awoke, he reached for the CD player at the side of his bed. The disc in the machine was *Koop Soup*, the only album recorded by local musician Jonas Koop before his mysterious disappearance. The album's 13 tracks seemed to amplify Marv's brain, translating his own thoughts into sound. If only he could lie there forever, bathing in its noise. Music kept demons at bay. In its presence, he never felt alone—although the silence between songs was unbearable.

He got up and walked to the window. Through the drizzle, seven storeys down, he saw Mr Reed drive past. Yawning, Marv turned away and found his notebook. Sitting back on the bed, he started to write:

Some Interesting Ways in Which I Might Die
Whilst strolling through a city, someone drops a pea from atop a large skyscraper. The pea hits me on the head.

He had read somewhere that when an object as innocuous as a pea is dropped from a very tall height, it can gain enough momentum to tear a skull asunder. He didn't know if it was true, but it sounded like a splendid way to go.

2. Whilst vomiting, I throw up all my insides (including my skeleton) and collapse in a mushy pile.

Marv often felt queasy.

3. A visit to the local biscuit factory ends in disaster when I plunge into the mix.

4. A dinosaur smashes through my window and tramples me into the carpet.

Marv peered cautiously at the window, then continued his dreams of death.

5. A barber snips off my head with extra-large scissors.

He was getting silly now.

6. Overweight, I fall asleep whilst hanging upside down and choke in the folds of my own flesh.

7. I drown after learning the hard way: I am not Jesus Christ; I cannot walk on water.

Ever since his mother's suicide, he ached to join her. He fantasised about his own corpse being discovered. He wondered who in this world was destined to find him. Whoever it was, he envisioned them reading the secret thoughts in the notebook beside his body. He imagined his words being posthumously published. The world would surely love him then; it was easier to love the dead.

Marv was always looking for love. The townspeople, on the other hand, only pursued sex. Not as a loving communication between two kindred souls, but as a barbaric, uncaring ritual that occasionally happened after drinking too much.

The woman for Marv was out there somewhere, beyond this maze of streets. Someday, she would pluck him from the gloom and save his life. Until then, he poured his soul into his notebook.

He decided to set off early for the job centre. Sliding into torn jeans and sneakers, he gathered his job seeker's paraphernalia, put on his duffel coat and left the flat.

Concrete and steel; spray paint and smashed glass; he walked to the bus stop as if the surrounding air had teeth.

7. MRS REED

Down the road, Mr Reed returned home. Helping his wife from the car, he carried her over the threshold and up to the bedroom. She felt light as a feather.

"There, there, Mrs Reed. Time for your beauty sleep."

Mr Reed had managed to doze in the car, where he'd dreamt of Joyce Burke.

Oh, Joyce. A real woman. Not like the thing in his arms. The thing he called Mrs Reed. She was a parody of womanhood in a big black wig, with button eyes and raggedy limbs.

He'd created her himself, stitching by moonlight on sleepless nights. Her crumpled face was crudely sewn; her arms and legs were just rolled-up bits of cloth. She had creased newspapers for guts and pipe cleaners for fingers.

He'd garbed her in a brown floral dress from the local charity shop. "For my wife," he'd insisted, when buying it. He remembered how the shop assistant looked at him as he touched the old brown dress. "Why are you looking at me like that?" He liked the feel of certain fabrics. That's all.

Whirling Mrs Reed around the bedroom, he cooed: "Oh, Joyce. I love you. When shall I ever see you again?"

A wife of rags could take no offence, yet there was something sad in its black button eyes, the way they stared so blindly ahead.

23

Placing the doll on the bed, he suddenly froze.

Something had moved inside the wardrobe.

Throwing open the doors, he peered inside.

But nothing stirred.

Closing the wardrobe, he turned to his wife. "I need to go into town for some supplies. I'll be back before you know it, darling."

After kissing her stuffed-stocking head, he picked a stray bit of fluff from his lips. Then he left the house, whistling tunelessly and dreaming of Joyce.

8. BUSES

Marv climbed aboard the bus. The driver was rude to him, naturally. Ripping his ticket from the machine, Marv noticed Joyce Burke, slumped on the back seat of the lower deck, looking tired and ratty.

The smell of piss stung Marv's nose as he made his way upstairs, clinging to the sticky metal supports. He wanted to sit in his favourite seat (front left, top deck), but the Sweet Guzzler had beaten him to it.

The Sweet Guzzler was Marv's arch-nemesis: an elderly man in flat cap and mackintosh, who stunk of pipe tobacco, and guzzled hard-boiled sweets from a paper bag on his knees. He and Marv were always in competition for the front left-hand seat on the top deck.

Flopping into a vacant seat behind the old man, Marv tried to ignore the Sweet Guzzler's noises: The *rustle, rustle* of the bag; the *clack, chomp, slurp* of his dentures. It drove Marv mad. He'd read somewhere that if you concentrated hard enough, you could alert someone's attention by demanding it telepathically. He had tried it before, standing at the window of his seventh storey flat, calling out in his mind for people to notice him. But no one ever did.

Marv concentrated on the back of the Sweet Guzzler's little white head. *Hear me, Sweet Guzzler. Get out of my seat and stop making stupid noises.* But the old man barely twitched.

Marv turned his attention, instead, to the flyblown window. Through his doleful reflection, the grey, blurry town passed by.

Beneath the pallid sky, rusted railings dripped cold rain, whilst industrial workplaces lay in wait like iron monsters. Rolls of barbed wire slithered atop walls, where peeling posters screamed of lost pets. Goblin children huddled at the ends of every alley, their young, spitting faces hardened like old men: Old men in tracksuits, with their caps on backwards.

Marv imagined himself as his fabulous alter ego, Marvellous Marvo, flying above the town. All the people below waved up and smiled, hailing the hero as he whizzed by.

Amid the crowd, one shrouded figure stood out. It was his mother, gently smiling and willing him on. He gave a salute, then flew onward, scenting the air for danger.

It wasn't long before he found it. Beth Anderson was squirming in the arms of her lecherous boyfriend, Darren Thompson. A crowd stood around, gawping and gasping, as Beth screamed and Darren laughed.

"Marv, help me!"

"Don't worry, Beth. I'm here."

Swooping down, he lifted her out of the villain's embrace.

Everyone cheered—apart from Darren, who could only shake his fist in impotent rage.

As Marv soared away, Beth planted a tender kiss upon his cheek, hugging herself close to his body.

Craaaaack.

Marv was awoken from his revery by the sound of skeletal branches slapping the window. His arms were empty, he no longer flew, and his underwear was stuck up his ass—but the Sweet Guzzler was alighting.

With his arch-nemesis gone, Marv was in the front left-hand seat quicker than a toupée on a windy day. He felt like an emperor in the throne of his golden chariot—a chariot with squeaking wheels. A sick little glow fluttered in his heart as the bus pulled away once more.

Before visiting the job centre, there would be time to visit Tony's Grotto. He hadn't been there in a while and, having some loose change in his pocket, he had a desire to find new, old treasure.

Marv leaned back and smiled. There was something about bus journeys he liked. They made him feel like he was going somewhere.

9. THE SWEET GUZZLER

The Sweet Guzzler, whose real name was Eric, stepped off the bus and into his home. Removing his flat cap and mackintosh, he hung them carefully on a peg in the hallway. He never bothered locking the door; he hadn't needed to in the past, why should he now?

As usual, the postman had delivered only one letter. Picking it up, he shuffled into the living room. His home was a faded brown blur, sparsely furnished and cold without Doris. He looked at her portrait atop the TV, her sepia smile, dark lashes and curls. He'd just been to lay fresh flowers on her grave.

He popped another sweet in his mouth. Not only did they remind him of Doris, but also his wartime friends, the American GIs, who'd introduced him to imported candies from the USA. They'd also introduced him to colourful slang words, which he remembered and smiled. That was back when he was a soldier; when this town still recognised there was a world beyond it. The only reminder of that now was the war monument, but its messages were smothered in graffiti and drunks.

The war had taken most of his friends. It seemed senseless killing each other. But history repeats itself, and no one ever learns.

He opened the post. He knew what it was. The council wanted him to find new accommodation so they could knock down his house and build another supermarket. There was a lovely new tenement block on the outskirts of town. Why didn't he move there?

Eric threw the letter in the bin. He wasn't going anywhere, nor would he give in to their threats (they were still demanding to know why Doris hadn't paid any tax in the last 23 years. The fact that she was dead wasn't good enough, apparently).

They'll have to knock the place down about my ears, Eric thought, whilst wondering what to do next. *Maybe I should watch a movie?* He and Doris loved the movies. All those black-and-silver ones, with real actors, strong storylines, and a hero and heroine embracing as the credits rolled. He'd never known any greater joy than holding her hand in a darkened theatre.

He placed a CD in the stereo: a collection of his favourite composer, Ludwig van Beethoven. He also loved Tchaikovsky, Bach and, when he was feeling more adventurous, Stravinsky. Sitting back in his favourite armchair, he let the music wash over him, chomping more sweets from the crumpled bag on the armrest.

Suddenly, Roland, his beloved black cat, leapt onto his lap, purring gently. "We are great friends, you and I," Eric smiled, his liver-spotted hands at rest in its fur.

Beethoven's eighth piano sonata rang out from the stereo. The haunting melodies conjured memories: Eric was young again. There had never been any war. All of his friends were alive. And Doris was in his arms.

A tear rolled down his cheek. And Ludwig van ferried him safely to Dreamland.

When he awoke, the music was over. His eyes were gummy, and Roland was gone.

"Oh, I'm sorry," he muttered to no one. "I must have nodded off."

Rubbing his eyes, he placed another sweet in his mouth. Then he saw the shadow figure, hunched upon the wall.

He should have locked the front door. But they would only have got in through the window.

The shadow advanced. It held Roland in one hand, and in the other . . .

The sweet in the old man's mouth slid to the back of his throat. He fell onto his knees, choking and dribbling. And when the cold blade slid across his throat, all of his problems were over.

10. TONY

With his guitar strapped on, Tony gave his appearance one last check in a backstage mirror. Here, he had two eyes: blue and gleaming. Stepping onto the stage, he was met with a roar of appreciation from the crowd.

A cannon-like explosion of drums announced the opening number. The female backing vocalists sashayed, lips pouting, and Tony's sausage-like fingers caressed his guitar strings with an agility that wakefulness stole.

Glorious chords poured out from the amps: The music of Tony's invention; his longing transformed into sound.

He stepped up to the mic and started to sing. His voice drenched the audience like a mighty sunray. They were all here: every woman he had ever loved, who had never loved him back. Rubbing slender shoulders alongside the likes of Rita Hayworth, Maureen O'Hara and Beryl Flynn were less ethereal beauties like Sylvia and Muriel from accountancy college, and, last but not least, his mother.

None of them looked at him with that squint of revulsion he had grown so accustomed to. Instead, they all screamed out his name. Tears streamed down their fabulous cheekbones, their angel eyes welling with desire. They swooned and fainted in a fanatical heave, writhing suggestively to the provocative beat.

It was Tony's music they loved. And, through it, they loved Tony.

They looked up at him as he'd once looked at them.

Tony never wanted to wake up.

And then he woke up.

11. IN THE GROTTO

Tony had fallen asleep behind the counter. He was awoken by the little bell tinkling on the shop door.

Oh, God, he thought, *a customer.*

Standing in the doorway, Marv didn't know where to begin. Tony's Grotto (actually *Tony's Grot*—amusing vandals had made away with the final *T* and *O*) was a treasure trove. Pillars of books, DVDs and used CDs rose from the floor as if they had been planted there and grown. Every square inch of the walls was covered with colourful posters and rare record covers.

At the centre of this maze stood Tony: Overweight, over-50, and over-balding (every lank strand of hair on his head was as rare as some of the records filling the racks). He had a bulbous nose, thick purple lips and brown stubs for teeth. His glass eye glinted in the shabby gloom. Stuffed in its baggy socket, the eye was too large for his head; jaundiced flesh hung round it like melting rubber. His real eye had been scratched out and eaten by a stray black cat when he was 27. His mother had always warned him to keep away from the graveyard. He never disobeyed her again.

"Can I help you, lad?"

"Just browsing," said Marv.

Eyeing the racks, he spotted a 12-inch copy of *Presenting the Fabulous Ronettes*. He and Beth used to sing their songs at school. On checking the price tag, though, he put the album straight back down. £272. He didn't realise it was *that* rare. Then he flicked through the other records and got an even bigger surprise.

The Beach Boys' *Pet Sounds*: £727.

A Collection of Beatles Oldies: £2,720.

Something Else by the Kinks: £7,270.

"Are you sure I can't help you, lad?"

Looking up, Marv noticed a signed photograph on the wall behind the shop owner's head. When he realised who it was, he gasped. "Is that Jonas Koop?"

Tony glared at Marv: "How has a whippersnapper like *you* heard of Jonas Koop?"

"*Koop Soup* is my favourite album," said Marv. "A girl at school copied it for me. We sang Koop's songs all the time." In a cracked voice, he began to sing "Will There Really Be a Morning?"—a Koop classic.

"Enough," Tony barked.

But Marv was enthused. "It was the first music I heard that really *moved* me. Those songs really spoke to my soul. Not like the stuff you hear today: soulless noise."

Tony hunched down close and Marv got a whiff of his pungent breath. "Come downstairs with me, lad. There's something I want to show you."

12. THE BALLAD OF JONAS KOOP

"A brick?"

Marv stood in Tony's basement, looking at a brick. It was placed upon a small table, as if it was something to be admired.

"No ordinary brick," said Tony. "This is from the back wall of the Fox & Newt pub. I kicked it off myself."

Marv found his confusion hard to articulate. Tony kept on talking: "I was a young man then: 25. I still had two eyes. Twenty-seven years ago it was. The night of Koop's final gig at the pub. He had just released his first album, *Koop Soup,* which he put out himself. Not many people bought it back then, but I was one of the lucky few who appreciated its magic. I felt certain that the rest of the world would soon catch up, and Koop would be launched as a global star. Someone this town could be proud of. But it wasn't to be."

Marv shook his head. "He was only 27."

"The magic number," Tony nodded. "Ever since Robert Johnson sold his soul to the Devil, all the greats have gone at that age: Hendrix, Morrison, Joplin, Cobain. Death is the price they pay for immortality. But at least they all enjoyed their moment of fame. Not like Koop."

"The paper said he ran away, because no one recognised his genius," Marv added. "They said he had a drug problem. That he couldn't cope."

"Koop never took drugs," snapped Tony. "But he did like the occasional tipple. I know because he was slightly drunk when I met him."

"What happened?"

"Before the gig, I was outside the pub, having a cigarette. When, all of a sudden, there he was, staggering towards me in a snazzy new leather jacket: Jonas Koop! I told him how much I loved his music; that I knew he would be big very soon. And he smiled and handed me a signed photograph—the one on the wall upstairs. Then he took a piss against the back of the pub, leaning against the wall. And that," Tony pointed to the brick, "is one of the very bricks he pissed on. I kicked it off myself!" Tony seemed very pleased with himself. "If you look closely, you can still see faint traces of urine."

Marv looked at the brick. It did look slightly damp in places, but it was still only a brick. "I'm due at the job centre," he said, turning for the stairs.

"I know what really happened to Koop."

Marv froze.

Tony stared into the brick. "There weren't many people at the gig that night. Less than 20, I'd say. And I was the only one there for the music. The others just wanted to get drunk and play dominoes.

"When Koop finally took to the stage, alone with his guitar, he looked scared at first. Then, all of a sudden, there's a glow in his eyes. He opens his mouth to sing. And the magic happens. Sounds just as he does on the record. Only better. He launches into 'Made-Up Girl'. Fantastic. And I'm there, bopping away at the bar with my pint.

"But when I look around, no one else is listening. They're *still* just playing dominoes and darts, supping their ale. *How can they be so oblivious?* They were completely unmoved. Anyway, *I* decided to enjoy myself. He plays two more: 'Will There Really Be a Morning?' and 'It Only Hurts When I Cry'. I'll never forget. And then someone pipes up. An old man sat on his own. *Why don't you shut that racket up?* he says. And everyone claps and cheers. *We don't want you here,* someone else says.

"Koop smiles politely. He's a gentleman, you see. He just gets ready for his next song. But there is no next song. They all stand up. Everyone in the pub. Men and women. Some old, some young. They all stand there, slow clapping. And then they all climbed onto the stage, laughing and jeering. *You don't belong here,* they kept saying. It was only a small stage; didn't look big enough to hold them all. Someone throws a punch. Koop tries to leave, but they push him to the ground. *Help,* he cries. *Help!*

"I was scared. What could I do? I tried to say something, but they were much louder than me. I looked to the landlord, Malc, for help, but he just shook his head and joined in. They grabbed Koop. Some had his legs; some had his arms. And they dragged him outside.

"I ran after them. They carried him down to the river. I couldn't see what they were doing. It was dark. They were huddled round him, laughing. I could still hear him yelling for help. Screaming, like I've never heard a man scream before in my life. And I was frozen on the spot, terrified. All I could do was watch." Tony's shoulders sagged. "All I could do was watch."

Marv started to back away. He was late for signing on.

"Someone took out a knife," Tony sniffed. "And they stabbed him, again and again. They all took turns. Passing the bloody blade from hand to hand. Laughing like hyenas." Wiping his nose on his arm, Tony walked over to an ornate box in the corner.

"Please don't tell me you've got his corpse in there," Marv stammered.

"They threw his body into the river," said Tony, reaching into the box.

Phew.

"But they cut off his head."

Marv couldn't believe what Tony pulled out from the box.

It still had hair: black and greasy. The dangling face was ripped. Tatters of waxy, yellow flesh clung to the greying bones. The eyeless sockets were full of dust, pouring down like powdered tears. There was something that passed for a nose . . .

Marv loved peculiar things, but this was too much. He turned and ran up the stairs, as Tony's voice boomed behind him.

"After they threw his body into the river, they played football with his head. Once they'd had enough, they kicked it away, and went back inside the pub. Back to their drink and their dominoes. I found the head by a tree. So, I picked it up and took it home. Don't know why. Same reason I kicked off the brick, I suppose. Do you want to hold the head?"

But Marv was gone. On hearing the bell tinkle above, Tony put the head of Jonas Koop back in its box. Then he got back to repricing his records.

13. GARAGE

Beth's eyes felt like smudges in her face. She'd been up most of the night, thinking. Zipping up her parka, she walked down the hill towards town. As she wasn't working at the off-licence until late afternoon, she had time to try and sort out her love life.

Her parents had known something was wrong. They always did.

"Go and sort it out, love," her mother had said.

Mr Anderson agreed: *"Darren's a good lad. It'd be a shame to see it end."*

Darren's a good lad. Everyone said that, not just her folks. So why was he never good to her?

There must be something wrong with me.

Passing the cemetery, a black-clad figure jumped out and grabbed her arm. She froze. A white face peered close to hers, hard eyes squinting through flaky skin. "The day of atonement is coming," the figure hissed, spittle spraying from his chapped lips.

"Oh, piss off." Beth pushed the man away. He fell against the gates, shaking the rain from their coils. "You'll be sorry," he shouted after her. "You'll *all* be sorry."

Beth turned and gave him the finger.

"Lesbian!" he cried.

Beth had no time for zealots. She walked on, down the cobbled alleys, until she reached the shops. Joyce Burke was outside the freezer centre, bottle necks protruding from her bag.

"Hello, Beth. Going to see your young man? I hear you've been having problems."

"How did you . . .?"

Joyce disappeared inside the shop, her bag clinking. Beth leaned against the war monument. *You can't even fart in this town without everybody turning around and sniffing the air.*

Over the road was Thompson Motors. Taking a deep breath, she crossed over and went inside.

Darren was working on an engine, his head beneath the bonnet. Beth imagined him as a circus performer, with his head inside a lion's mouth. Her eyes wandered to the walls, the ghastly pin-ups from *Minge* magazine.

"Morning," came a cheery voice from behind. It was Benny, Darren's co-worker. He bounded into the garage, clutching two bacon sandwiches. He gave Beth a wink. "If I'd known you were coming, love, I would have got you one."

Beth smiled. "It's all right, Ben. I'm not hungry."

"Where the hell have you been?" Darren emerged from under the bonnet, glaring at Benny.

"Sorry, Daz. I got talking to Janice at the café."

"Who gives a fuck?" Darren snatched his sandwich then turned to Beth. "What do you want? I'm busy."

"Well . . . I . . ."

Beth looked at Benny. He could have been her boyfriend's twin, what with their matching coveralls and shaven heads. But Benny was shorter and less wiry, and he had much kinder eyes. "Do you guys want to be alone?" he said, between mouthfuls of bacon.

"No," said Darren. "It's all right."

Beth sighed. There wasn't much she could say in Benny's presence. And Darren knew it.

"I'll come back later," she muttered.

Trudging to the door, she tripped on a coil of rope. She could feel the boys laughing behind her, but when she looked back, they both looked serious. Darren shuffled towards her, flecks of brown sauce round his mouth. "What time do you finish work tonight?"

"Eight-thirty," Beth replied.

"I'll meet you after, then. At the pub."

"Okay," said Beth. Perhaps there was some hope.

"Did you say we're meeting at eight-thirty?" said Benny.

Perhaps not.

"Can I come, too?" Darren's father, Mr Thompson, slid out from under a car, his moustache and coveralls stained with oil.

"Bloody hell, Dad! How long have you been there?"

Father Thompson rolled back under and chortled. "I hear everything."

For fuck's sake. Beth turned and stalked through the door, being careful not to trip over the rope this time. Darren came out behind her. "And don't wear that stupid coat tonight," he said. "It makes you look like a freak."

"Hey," she said. "I like this stupid coat."

But Darren was distracted. "Oi, oi," he whispered. "What have we here?"

Looking up the road, Beth saw a familiar figure hurtling towards them. It was Marv, her old friend from school.

"Don't hurt him, Darren," she said.

14. STARVING MARVIN

Running to the job centre, Marv couldn't get the dead grey head of Jonas Koop out of his mind. He tried to reassure himself that it was just a prop; that he'd been the victim of a grisly prank.

It's obvious that Tony is losing his mind: overpricing his stock; obsessing over the number 27 . . .

"Oi! Starving Marvin!"

Marv's thoughts were halted by a familiar cry. He'd reached Thompson Motors. Darren was standing outside the garage with his accomplice, Benny.

Oh no. Decapitated heads are more appealing than those two.

But then Marv saw Beth. Unable to even look at her old friend, she loitered by the garage doors as Darren and Benny marched forward.

"Oi, Starving Marvin. We're talking to you."

Marv would never forgive Darren for taking Beth away; for forcing cheese into his mouth when he was allergic to it; for throwing away his mother's book and pushing him through a hedge the night of the end-of-school dance . . .

"Where do you think you're going, gay boy?"

Darren and Benny now stood before him, their grinning shaven heads in stark contrast to his own unruly mop. He tried to shuffle past, but the brawny mechanics blocked his way.

"We said, where are you going?"

"Nowhere," Marv mumbled.

"Nowhere isn't a place, dick head," said Benny.

That's what you think, thought Marv. He looked down at a rain puddle. "I'm late for the job centre."

"Fucking dole scum," said Darren. "Why don't you get a job?"

"I'm trying," said Marv.

"Fucking pussy."

"Where's your bra, Marvin?" Benny started prodding Marv's duffle coat. "Under here somewhere?"

"Marvin's a gay boy," Darren sneered.

"Yeah," said Benny. "Always reading books."

Marv scrunched his face. "How does that make me gay?"

"Well, you don't have a girlfriend," said Darren.

"I can't help it if girls don't like me," Marv squeaked.

Darren and Benny howled with laughter. Marv flushed. He wished he'd kept his mouth shut.

"Hey, Daz," said Benny. "Remember that time when you made him eat cheese?"

"Yeah," Darren smirked. "He couldn't stop farting. Stunk out the classroom. Everyone was laughing."

Marv still heard that laughter.

"It's all right, Starving Marvin," Darren cooed. "There's no cheese today. But we do have bacon." He threw the remainder of his sandwich into Marv's face. It bounced off his nose, leaving a splodge of brown sauce. Marv raised his sleeve to wipe it off.

"Did you just try and hit me, freak?"

"No. I was just rubbing my . . ."

"Just rubbing yourself, you fucking perv. And thinking of Beth. I've noticed the way you look at

45

her. At school, you used to follow her around like a dog with two dicks."

Marv's eyes returned to the puddle, his cheeks burning. Darren continued: "She told me you creep her out. She can't stand you. You make her feel sick."

"Leave him alone."

Marv looked up. It was Beth. She'd come to save him, at last.

"Piss off, Beth," said Darren.

"*You* piss off," said Beth.

Darren lifted his hand. "What did you say, bitch?"

"Don't you *ever* try and hit me." Beth squared up to him.

"Come on, love." Benny put his arm round her shoulder. "I'll put the kettle on." He started dragging her back towards the garage.

"Fuck you, Darren," Beth called back, as Benny led her inside.

"I'll deal with you later, bitch," Darren spat.

"Don't talk to Beth like that," said Marv.

"What did you say?" Darren's eyes blazed.

"Don't talk to *any* woman like that."

Darren gave Marv a shove. "What are you going to do about it, pussy?"

Before Marv could respond, Benny rushed out of the garage and threw something at him. A thick coil of rope looped over Marv's head and tightened round his stomach, pinning his arms to his sides.

Oh, dear God. What now?

15. THE CROWD

Darren and Benny stood at the end of the rope, grinning. They gave it a yank, and Marv stumbled forward, struggling for balance.

"Let's go for a little walk," said Darren.

They dragged Marv along the road like a dog on a leash, pausing before the war monument.

"Hey, everyone," Darren called out. "Come and have a look at the freak!"

Passers-by froze, staring at Darren and his woeful exhibit.

"Come and see the dole scum!"

It didn't take long for a crowd of about 30 or 40 people to gather. Their eyes seared into Marv as much as the rope. Tight round his middle, it squeezed the breath from his lungs.

"Look at that idiot," one onlooker observed.

The woman at his side laughed: "He looks bloody mental if you ask me."

Darren continued his spiel: "Come on, everybody! Look at the freak! This little twat takes our hard-earned tax then wastes his days weeping and wanking at our expense. What do you think of that?"

The crowd roared their disapproval. "I don't pay my taxes for you to weep and wank!" some old woman yelled, shaking a puckered fist.

"So, what are we gonna do about it?" Darren yelled.

There was a murmur among the crowd. "Fuck knows," said someone.

"I'll show you," said Darren. He clenched his fist and slammed it into Marv's nose.

The crowd laughed and cheered as Marv hit the ground. Benny yanked the rope and got him to his feet again.

Marv's head flopped forward, blood gushing from his nostrils.

"So, come on," said Darren. "Who's next?"

The crowd looked at one another. Then a small voice piped up. "I'll have a go." A little girl stepped out from behind the legs of her father. She couldn't have been older than nine.

"Come on then, darling," Darren smiled, as the little girl walked over.

She squinted up at Marv. "Your nose looks horrible. It's all busted."

Marv looked down at her with dripping eyes. Then the little girl kicked him hard in the shin and skipped back to her place in the crowd. Marv buckled at the knees, grimacing. He wanted to collapse, but Benny kept yanking the rope, keeping him on his feet. The crowd cheered.

"Go on then, I'll have a bash," said a red-faced old man.

Darren gestured for him to come forward. The old man rolled up his sleeves, spat into his hands, and swung a punch. Marv's head flew back with a crack.

"That's it! Chin him!" someone hissed from the crowd.

Marv crumpled to the ground. Benny tugged the rope, pulling him up like a broken puppet. Then he wrapped the rope around the war monument, tying Marv to the column.

The crowd laughed. Marv clenched his eyes, but it didn't make them go away. He felt like telling them that he'd twitched and mumbled in every ill-fitting suit he could borrow; that he'd walked the streets without tire, wearing down his one and only pair of scuffed shoes in search of work. But each time he faced the same disappointment.

His mouth parted to say something, but then narrowed to a soundless slit. It was no use. These people would just mock his every uttering, like birds picking at carrion.

"Come on," said Darren. "You can all have a go!"

One by one, the crowd put down their shopping bags and surged forward. They took turns, kicking and punching the boy on the war monument with all the strength their rage allowed. Children, urged on by their parents, kicked and giggled again and again. Heavy boots struck his ribs. Dentures bit his ears; rough tongues licked his face.

Suddenly a voice called out. "Stop it! You're hurting him!"

It was Beth, pushing her way through the heaving throng. Finding Darren, she latched onto his arm. "Can't you make them stop?"

Darren pushed her away, then punched Marv in the stomach once more.

"That's enough!" But Beth's plea was swallowed up by the crowd's animal roar.

She turned and fled from the awful scene, colliding with a moustachioed gentleman, shoving himself to the front. "What's going on here?"

Everyone stopped when they saw it was PC McGann, their most respected lawman.

"Are you all right, lad?" He took Marv's swollen face in his hands. The boy's eyes were purple mounds. Blood streaked down his head. "Answer me, boy."

The crowd fell silent. McGann tightened his grip on Marv's face, squeezing the lips into a blistered kiss. "Been a bad boy, have we?"

Marv could only groan.

McGann pushed Marv's head back down then stared at Darren. Darren looked away, arms hanging at his sides. Then the policeman nodded. "Carry on," he said. And, as he walked away, the people thundered in appreciation.

Around and around the war monument, the jeering crowd rotated: kicking, hitting and spitting like some nightmare carousel. All were united in their ire. Familiar faces, such as Mr Reed and Janice, the café owner, took part. Even Joyce Burke put her best foot forward and gave the boy a kick. But these individual faces were blurred through their violence, as if they were all just one limb of a wildly flailing body.

From the doorway of his Grotto, Tony observed the vicious horde with shame. Their noise had interfered with the record he was listening to. He wondered who the unfortunate victim was this time. Then he recognised the bloody heap tied to the war monument. It was the kid who had just left his shop; the one with whom he'd confided the truth of Jonas Koop. He went back inside, relieved that their brunt wasn't directed at him, as it had been in his youth. As it had been for Koop.

Turning his stereo louder, he lost himself in another world.

In the world outside, the crowd untied the lifeless body and carried it down to the river.

16. OLIVIA

Joyce arrived home later than usual. She'd been for a short walk after work, thinking things through. When she got in, Arthur was in the kitchen, routing through the bread bin. "It's almost half past six," he said. "Have you been looking for the cat again?"

"What if I have?" Joyce dumped her coat over the back of a chair.

Arthur sighed. "You'll never find it."

"How do *you* know?"

Arthur changed the subject. "Do you know where the plasters are?"

"Cut yourself again, have you?"

"Yes. On those new train tracks. The edges are quite sharp."

"You and your stupid toys." Joyce scowled as Arthur yanked at the drawers. "Stop pulling my kitchen apart. You're bleeding all over my spoons. There are bandages in the pantry, I think."

"Thanks," said Arthur. "I'll take a look."

As Arthur explored the pantry, Joyce poured herself a mugful of gin. It was half empty when Arthur emerged with a thin strip of bandage round his finger. "You were right, love. They were in the pantry."

"Well, hip-hip-hooray," said Joyce.

"Any chance of a bite to eat, love? I'm famished."

"Feed yourself. I can't do everything for you."

"Did you get those fish fingers this morning?"

His wife ignored him.

"Are they in the freezer?" He couldn't find them in there. Nor were they in the fridge. And he'd already looked inside the pantry. "I think I'll go and watch one of my train videos," he said, finally.

"Yes, fuck off back to your trains." Joyce downed the remainder of her gin. Then poured herself another as Arthur traipsed into the living room.

She leaned against the sink, clutching her mug. It had been a bad day. Not only was she still having problems with Wayne, the kid who said *twat* instead of *trois*, but she couldn't get that other boy out of her mind. *Marv, I think they called him.* She could still see him, tied to the war monument, screaming and bloody. Before work, she'd accompanied everyone else down to the river and watched them throw his body in. She knew it was the ritual, but it still didn't feel right somehow.

A loud rumble of thunder sounded in the sky; lightning flashes filled the kitchen. Joyce thought of Olivia; there had been a storm like this the night she was born.

Joyce could never forget the birth of her only child. Her waters had broken on this very kitchen floor. The whole ghastly business had been presided over by her whimpering husband, and that wretched black cat, hissing at the window, a third eye staring from inside its mouth.

She turned and opened the cupboard above the sink. There, next to the biscuit tin, was Olivia.

Joyce had always wanted a daughter. But the thing that had clawed, mewling from her womb, almost 30 years ago, was a monster. It looked more like a squid than a girl. A mess of mucus and tentacles. They called it Olivia, nonetheless, and kept it in a jar. (They'd got the jar from the pub; it had once housed pickled eggs.)

Joyce regarded her daughter's body, floating hairless and upright in the jar's murky fluid; its domed head and undeveloped features; its six slimy tentacles and wrinkled brown skin. One oily black eye glinted on the side of its face.

"Oh, Olivia," Joyce cried, hugging the jar to her bosom.

The shadow of a cat flickered across the kitchen wall. Joyce shrieked, dropping the jar.

It smashed.

Pickling fluid gushed across the linoleum. Olivia's tentacles twitched.

"No, Olivia. Stay where you are!" Joyce searched for the dustpan and brush, but she couldn't find it.

Olivia dragged herself across the kitchen floor on thick, swelling tentacles, leaving a trail of slime.

"Come back!"

Olivia slithered behind the washing machine. It was her favourite hiding place.

Best to leave her there, thought Joyce. *She'll come out when she's ready. Now, where is that dustpan and brush?* Joyce looked down at the shattered jar. *I'll clean it up later.*

She looked to the window. The black cat sat on the sill outside, glaring at Joyce through the rain-streaked glass. It could have been smiling.

As Joyce approached it, the cat leapt away and tore off down the street.

"Damn you!"

Joyce reached for her coat. It was only half-on as she raced from the house.

Arthur leaned against the hallway wall, watching his wife run out into the rain. As she slammed the front door, he went into the kitchen where he'd heard the jar smash from the living room. *Where does she keep the dustpan and brush?* He poked a finger through the jagged shards. *Oh, I don't know. I'll clean it up later.* He peered behind the washing machine.

"Hello, Olivia, love."

Olivia had spread her brown wet body over the back of the washing machine. She looked to be comfortable there. Arthur reached down. He felt a tentacle stroke his hand. "You know, if it was up to me, I wouldn't keep you in a jar?"

A small slick hole opened in the centre of Olivia's head. It was full of crooked little teeth. From behind the teeth, a meaty purple tongue flicked out.

"Are you hungry again, sweetheart?" Arthur spotted another slight cut on his finger, a bubble of blood swelling at its tip. *Must have been the broken jar.* Olivia gurgled, thick strands of drool dripping from her mouth. "Okay, love. I'll feed you."

Arthur bent down, holding his bleeding finger over Olivia's mouth. Her thin, crinkled lips clamped over it, the dense tongue lapping away at the blood, the mouth moving in and out as she sucked. Arthur looked down at the sad black eye staring up at him, then pulled his finger out with a moist *slurp*. "You mustn't take all of Daddy's blood, darling."

Olivia growled.

"I know, love. I'll have to find your mother now. She's very upset."

Arthur pulled his coat on over his pyjamas. "Maybe one day, you can play with Daddy on the trains in the attic? You'd like that, wouldn't you?"

Olivia burbled.

"Good girl. Okay, I'd better see to your mother. Good night, love. Sleep tight."

He left the house and went looking for his wife in the rain.

He found her moments later, perched, breathless, on an alleyway wall. "You couldn't find it?" he shouted above the storm.

Rain dripped from her jowls as she shook her head.

"Come on," he said, putting an arm about her shoulders. "Let's have an early night."

17. WALK

Having finished her shift at the off-licence, Beth pulled up the hood of her parka and began the long walk home. It was dark now and raining heavily.

Lightning flashed. Thunder rumbled.

She hadn't felt like working that afternoon, but she and her folks needed the money. Luckily, there had been few customers.

Huddled within her big green coat, Beth tried to forget the last couple of days. But that was as impossible as ignoring the damp chill of rain seeping in through her trainers.

The streets were surprisingly empty, with only the distant holler of a Friday night drunkard providing any sign of life.

If you could call it that.

Deep in her pocket, her cell phone bleeped. Darren had been calling repeatedly for the past half-hour.

I'm not going to answer. I don't want to see him right now. He'll be at the pub, getting wasted with his dad and Benny. Not a care in the world.

On reaching the closed-up garage, she crossed over to the war monument. Frayed strands of rope lay sodden at its base. The rain had washed all the blood away.

I hope you got home safely, Marv.

She remembered, when they were about 14, Marv used to cycle up the hill to her house with poems he'd written. Once he'd delivered them to her, he would just blush furiously then cycle off back down the hill. When she told her girlfriends about this, they all thought it was pretty strange. But Beth thought it was cute. And the poems weren't that bad. She just didn't feel attracted to him.

He was too nice.

She valued him as a friend, though. Until Darren came along.

But that's what happens in life, isn't it? What's that well-known phrase? The one John Lennon pinched off somebody else? "Life is . . ."

Lightning flickered overhead.

Passing the hotel, she remembered the end-of-school dance. The night had started out all right, but Darren had ended it by going off with her so-called friend, Francesca.

Why do I always go back to him? Because no one else could love me?

What about Marv?

I don't feel the same way.

Lost in her thoughts, Beth didn't see the pale, crusty hands reaching out through the cemetery gates. She only became aware of them as they covered her mouth, dragging her back.

Can't breathe.

Rough against her lips. The smell was like ammonia. Stinging her nose.

Can't breathe.

Can't—.

And then the darkness grew darker still.

18. BED

Joyce rolled over and looked at her husband.

How can he sleep?

His snores were louder than the thunder.

She looked to the bedside clock. *2:07 a.m.* Another hour had passed. Time didn't tick by this fast when she was working.

Oh well, at least it's Saturday now.

She and Arthur had first met on a Saturday, 25 years ago, when the local hotel still held dances. Joyce had fallen pregnant that very night. They had to get married for the sake of the child (the child that was still suckered to the back of the washing machine).

Joyce had never told Arthur that he wasn't the only man she'd danced with that night. The young Mr Reed had swept her off her feet and into the graveyard next door. After a moment's excitement against a gravestone, she pulled up her knickers and told him to "get lost". Reed duly complied, running away among the tombstones, clicking his heels. Then she went back inside the hotel and Arthur asked her to dance. Several lager shandies were followed by a fumbling bout of passion on his mother's sofa. Olivia could have been the child of either man. But Joyce believed it to be Arthur's, because she blamed him for everything. She often wondered what her life would have been like if she'd married Mr Reed instead.

The mattress creaked as she turned over once more. On the bedside table was a bottle of gin.

Only for emergencies, mind.

But now *was* an emergency. As was yesterday, and the day before.

Her husband never said anything about her drinking, but she knew he didn't approve. Taking the bottle, she got out of bed and walked over to the window. Rain spattered across the pane. A solitary streetlamp burned outside. But she could see no sign of the cat.

Lightning flashed.

She took a few slurps of gin straight from the bottle, before replacing it on the table and making her way to the adjoining bathroom.

Thunder rumbled.

She flushed the toilet several times, hoping the noise would wake her husband.

"God, I'm getting old," she told the bathroom mirror, before traipsing back to the bedroom. "Oh, you're awake, are you?"

Arthur was sitting up in bed. "Are you all right?"

She returned to the window.

"You're still looking for that cat, aren't you?" he sighed.

"What if I am?" she snapped.

"You know it's no good, love."

She turned to face him. "That black cat was there when Olivia was born."

"But that doesn't mean it sucked up her soul."

"Must you put it so crudely?"

"I'm sorry, I didn't . . ."

"When Olivia was born, the cat took her soul and made her a monster. It's voodoo—black magic, or something. I know. I've read about these things."

"But magic isn't real, darling."

"The cat had three eyes, remember? One was inside its mouth. It looked almost human. If it wasn't for that stupid cat, Olivia would be a normal little girl."

"She *is* a normal little girl."

"She has six legs!"

"I mean . . . can't we just be happy and love her, even if she has six legs?"

"You know we can't."

"Why? What does it matter? No legs, six legs, black, white, green: I'd love her just the same."

"You think you're so perfect, don't you?"

"But the cat you're looking for . . . after 25 years . . . it won't even be the same one."

"It *is* the same cat. It spoke to me. In Olivia's voice."

"Olivia doesn't have a voice."

"That's because the cat's got it, you fool!"

Arthur blinked. "You know, I've tolerated this for far too long. I've humoured you and gone along with your stories . . ." He paused when he saw his wife's face. He'd seen her look angry before, but never like this.

"You don't love Olivia," she hissed. "You just love your trains."

Arthur turned over. He was fast asleep as soon as his head hit the pillow.

"It's all so easy for you, isn't it?" she cried.

He answered with a loud and particularly irritating snore.

So, she went downstairs and grabbed a large hammer.

19. MR REED'S NEW JOB

Mr Reed drove slowly through the rain. Thunder roared and lightning lit his way. His wife sat beside him in the passenger seat. He didn't always bring her to work, but he'd had a bit to drink and was feeling sentimental.

The car hit a slight bump in the road and she slumped over, her cloth head hitting the dashboard. "Easy now," said Mr Reed, correcting her position.

Mr Reed loved his new job. He had never known what he was supposed to be doing in his previous occupation, running the old people's home; he was at an utter loss wiping backsides and pretending to care. He knew what he was doing in *this* job, though: He had to find the black cat. The one Joyce was always on about. It was the only way he could slide back into her affections. Those minutes of romance they shared in the graveyard so long ago had been the greatest moment of his life. Finding the cat would keep that moment alive. He didn't know why the cat was so important. Only that he should find it. Nor did he care that Joyce wasn't paying him for his work; he had his wife's disability allowance to keep him going.

Driving past the war monument, he saw three vagabonds huddling in a shop doorway for warmth. "Bloody tramps," he muttered. "Something will have to be done about them."

But not tonight.

It was 3:33 a.m. when he saw the black cat. It was sitting on a wall on the outskirts of town.

"There you are, you devil!"

He pulled over and patted his wife's arm. "Stay here, darling. I'll be right back."

Leaving the car, he ducked through the rain and crept over to where the cat was licking its paws.

Silly devil. I have you now.

Lightning crackled across the dark, early morning sky; thunder bellowed. Mr Reed pounced, grabbing the cat's slender body and running with it to the back of his car. He opened the boot and tossed the creature inside. After slamming the door shut, he looked down at his hands and saw long, red scratches running across the skin. He sucked at the blood, then peered around. No one was looking. Running back to the driver's side, he hopped in behind the wheel.

"Daddy's been hurt." He stroked his wife's stocking hand. "The devil scratched me. But I'll be all right. Daddy's a big, strong boy."

He started the car. "As soon as it's light, we'll go and see Joyce. She'll tell us if we've got the right one this time. But first," he yawned, "let's get some shut-eye; I'm knackered."

As he drove home, the cat hissed and writhed in the boot.

20. TRAINS

Arthur was awoken by a crash. He started from his bed. The noise had nothing to do with the storm; it was coming from the attic.

He shinned up the ladder as fast as he could—and there was Joyce, clutching a hammer. For the first time in their marriage, she was smiling at him. His beautiful trains lay smashed at her feet.

"My trains!"

Arthur clasped his head and wailed, dropping to his knees. He sobbed like a baby in an old man's body. She left him there, weeping amid the twisted tracks and smashed-up metal.

"How could you be so cruel?"

Climbing down from the attic, Joyce decided to give sleep one more try. There were still a few more hours left before sunrise.

As her head hit the pillow, it was free of tentacled children and useless husbands. She thought only of Mr Reed.

I hope he waits for me.

Minutes later, on cloudy grounds, she danced alone in Dreamland.

21. LIKELY LADS

Darren and Benny tumbled into the garage a little after four a.m. They were laughing and clutching doner kebabs.

"Shhh!" Darren held up a finger. "You'll wake Dad." (Mr Thompson had left the pub hours earlier and was now asleep in the flat upstairs.)

"Whatever you say, darling." Benny shoved Darren against a car bonnet, then planted a slobbering kiss on his mouth.

"Gerroff me, you queer." Darren pushed him away.

"What's wrong with you?" said Benny.

"Nothing."

"Come on, Daz. I know when something's wrong."

"*Look . . .*" On rising from the bonnet, Darren staggered drunkenly, twisting his ankle. He dropped to the floor, kebab and all. "Ow," he winced, biting his lip. "Now look what you made me do."

"Soz, Daz." Benny crouched beside him.

"Fuck off."

"Look, if you don't tell me what's wrong, I'll . . ."

"All right, all right. Keep your voice down. It's just, you know, Marv. Earlier."

"Starving Marvin? What about him?"

"We killed him, you div."

"So?"

"Well, don't you feel bad?"

"It wasn't just us, you know? Everyone killed him."

"I know, but . . ."

"Look, he didn't fit in. The majority didn't want him here. So, we made it happen. It's democracy, innit."

"Yeah."

"So, why are you still looking like a slapped arse?"

Darren pulled his phone from his pocket. "I'm going to call Beth again."

"Forget that bitch." Benny grabbed the phone.

"Gerroff my phone!" But Darren was too drunk to put up a fight; he couldn't get off the floor.

"She had her chance to come and meet us tonight," said Benny. "And she blew it. If she really cared, she'd have answered earlier."

"Suppose you're right," Darren slurred.

"I am right."

"You're always right. Now give me back my phone."

Benny raised it above his head. "You'll have to get it off me."

Darren made a few feeble lunges from the floor, then fell back. "I'm too drunk."

Benny put the phone down and squeezed Darren's balls.

"Ow, gerroff me, you queer!"

Benny let go.

"What did you do that for?"

"Just making sure you've got some bollocks," said Benny. "And I like touching your dick."

"Fuck off."

"You fuck off."

"No, *you* fuck off."

Benny grabbed a handful of meat from his kebab and slapped it into Darren's face.

"Oi, you tosser!"

It was Benny's turn to shush Darren. "You don't want to wake your dad."

"You fucker."

Benny grinned. "Let me clean if off for you."

He started licking chilli sauce from Darren's face. "Gerroff."

"You like it, really," said Benny.

Darren laughed.

Benny kissed him again. This time, Darren didn't push him away: He pulled down his tracksuit bottoms and said, "I love you, you fucker."

Benny rolled over and smiled: "I know."

22. AWAKE

Beth opened her eyes to darkness. A musty stench hit her nose; like dust and rotting meat.

Where am I?

Her back hurt and she couldn't move her arms. She felt woozy and cold.

Looking down, she saw black strips of fabric criss-cross her body through jagged holes, binding her to something hard and wooden. Shatters of stained glass lay at her feet amid piles of ash. Long, boarded-up windows stared down.

Her groggy eyes slowly adjusted. A dank stone archway loomed ahead. From its apex there hung a giant cross, on which a skinny, bearded man bled with eyes and mouth agape. At first, Beth thought the man was real, but then she noted the chipped flecks of paint all over his body. Below the cross was an altar, smothered in grime.

She was at the end of some kind of bench or pew. Someone was sitting close beside her.

Despite the ache in her neck, she slowly turned her head and said "Hello" through chattering teeth.

But the figure didn't respond; just sat there hunched, flies buzzing round its head.

Squinting, she could see peeling flakes of skin on the stranger's downturned face.

Beth tried to rise, but she was bound so tight that her ties sawed into her flesh.

"What's going on? Where am I?" she cried. "Darren? Benny? Is this some kind of a joke?"

Then she fell silent. Something was scraping its way towards her from behind.

23. SATURDAY MORNING

Joyce got out of the shower, humming to herself. She felt refreshed. Arthur was still in the attic with his broken toys. She could hear him wailing as she put on her make-up.

"Quiet up there," she yelled. Nothing was going to ruin her morning.

It was still early. Not yet six a.m.

She went downstairs to the kitchen then halted before the smashed jar on the floor.

I'll get Arthur to clean it up later.

Stepping over the broken glass, she peered behind the washing machine. Olivia was still there. It looked like she was sleeping.

She'll come out when she's ready.

Through net curtains, Joyce watched the sky turn from black to grey. Then she caught her reflection.

Who do you think you are? Lipstick and eyeshadow can't hide your sagging features.

With a squashed heart, she reached for the gin.

24. SHELTER

Beth squirmed as the scraping footsteps grew nearer. She couldn't turn her head enough to see who or what they belonged to, but she was able to observe several others sitting in the pews behind. Like the person sat beside her, they were still and silent, hunched in the shadows, infested by flies. She kept pushing at her tethers, trying to break free. But it was no good.

As the footsteps sounded by her side, their owner bumped against her and limped past, dragging a clubfoot shoe. She could see it was a man, clad entirely in black. Once he'd reached the front, he turned before the altar, and Beth recognised him as the strange old man who had accosted her yesterday. His pale face seemed to glow in the dark; his eyes were hard glints in a sea of scabs; his lean mouth was not designed to smile. He held up his hands for silence, even though there was an abundance of quiet.

"Dearly beloved," he began, his voice a stentorian rasp, "we are gathered here today for shelter. May our Lord forgive and protect us in His home—for the day of atonement has come."

25. GIN

Joyce stumbled upstairs. A near-empty gin bottle swung from her left hand. Her right arm scraped along the wallpaper, steadying her ascent.

"Arthur," she slurred. "Arthur."

A mist brimmed over her eyes. She saw only the blurred dark browns of the house. Her head felt 10 times heavier than the rest of her.

Stumbling across the landing, she began to climb the attic ladder. The bottle clunked on every rung; her feet kept slipping off. But, eventually, she reached the top, and dragged herself through the trap.

Arthur lay curled amid his broken toys, clutching a dinted train to his breast. He looked just like a baby with a teddy bear, she thought. Crawling towards him, she continued to call his name.

"Arthur."

Exhaling loudly, she flopped down on top of his body and began to laugh.

"Arthur."

Her breath blew round his face, a stinking wind. He twitched and snored, lost in a dream.

"Arthur."

She rolled the glass bottle across his face, chortling as it squashed his nose.

"Play with me, Arthur."

Pulling at his pyjama bottoms, she flicked his limp penis.

"I'm lonely."

His snores ripped through her ears.

"Come on. It's as easy as one, two, three. It's as easy as . . . une, deux, *twat* . . ."

With her free hand, she reached between her legs and started rubbing against him.

"Une, deux, *twat*."

Her other hand tapped his sleeping face with the bottle.

"Wake up, Arthur. You . . . une, deux, *twat*."

Raising the bottle higher, she dropped it onto his head, causing an amusing *thunk* sound. Giggling, she raised the bottle again and slammed it down harder, making a louder, funnier noise. Then she did it again.

He stopped snoring. The glass cracked. Her eyes filled with tears. Her head screamed with noise.

"Une, deux, TWAT! Une, deux, TWAT!"

She thrust the broken bottle in rhythm with her cries, stabbing until the glass fell apart in shards.

Blood sprayed across the attic walls, dripping from his smashed-up toys, staining the floor.

Then there was stillness; an agonising quiet.

What have I done?

She hugged his carcass.

"I'm sorry."

She pressed her wet face against his cold, slashed skin.

"I love you. I love you."

And then, from downstairs, she heard the doorbell ring.

26. CONGREGATION

On the other side of town, Beth remained captive. She'd tried screaming out, but the old man before her was completely oblivious, mired in his sermon:

"And the Lord built the town upon the back of a serpent. Tired of being stomped on, the serpent will now raise its head and bite. And we will all suffer the consequences."

What is he yapping about?

She continued to squirm and pull at her tethers. But she wasn't making any progress.

"The day of atonement is here!"

With palms upraised, the old man lifted his glistening eyes to the crucified effigy above.

"Oh, dear Lord. Please have mercy on our wretched souls. We have ignored you for so long, and now we beg forgiveness."

As if in answer, the giant crucifix wobbled, then fell. The base of the cross pierced the old man's midriff, pinning him to the floor. Blood bubbled from the corners of his mouth; his bone-white hands clawed at the air.

"Repent," he croaked. "Repent!"

Beth pulled even harder at her ties, ignoring the pain this caused. The old man hobbled to his feet like a half-crushed insect, the crucifix protruding from his body. A shower of stones rained down from above.

The roof is caving in!

Through the falling masonry, Beth glimpsed a shadow behind the altar.

I know you . . .

Seconds later, it was gone. And Beth returned to the crashing sounds of plummeting concrete, and the old man's breathless screams.

I need to get out of here . . .

"Repent!"

The old man staggered forward, nosediving towards her.

Shit!

Weighed down by the giant crucifix, he went crashing through the front pew, squashing the mute, hunched figure at her side.

Jolting to a slant, Beth saw that she had become separated from the rest of the pew, and, although she was still attached to the end of it, she was, at least, able to stand.

Looking around, she saw great slabs of brickwork plunging to the floor, creating plumes of dust.

How do I get out? I can barely see . . .

Just to her right, something flickered; a grimy reflection in the air.

You again . . .

"Who are you?" Beth moved slowly.

It's not easy to walk with the end of a pew tied to your ass . . .

"Is that . . .?"

As bricks smashed down around her, she finally reached the shadowy figure.

"Marv! I'm glad you're all right. I'm sorry about what happened to you. I tried to stop them, but . . ."

Marv observed her with sad, sallow eyes. "I'm late for the job centre," he said. Although up-close, his voice sounded distant.

"Are you all right?" Beth reached out to him, but her fingers touched an old wooden door. As it creaked open, she tripped down some cracked, stone steps.

Shocked by the daylight, she tumbled through a bramble bush, then landed upright on her smashed-up pew.

With wide eyes, she watched the ancient building cave in before her, burying the old man and his silent spectators. Clouds of gritty vapour rose as the rubble sank.

Deep within the brambles, she heard one final scream:

"Dear Lord! No—"

Silence.

Beth caught her breath and squinted. She was on a patch of grass with rows of tombstones on either side.

I'm in the cemetery.

Her cell phone went off in her pocket, but her arms were still strapped to her sides.

At least I'm alive.

Just as she was thinking things couldn't get worse, it started to rain.

27. INTRUSION

The doorbell wouldn't stop ringing.

Joyce looked at her watch. *It's half past eight in the morning. Who could it be at this time?*

Whoever it was, they weren't going away.

Best see who it is. Act normal.

Biting back tears, Joyce left her dead husband in the attic and crept downstairs. She'd never felt more sober in her life.

Pretend that nothing has happened. No one must suspect . . .

Ambling down the hallway, blood dripped from her shaking hands; wiping the tears from her eyes, she left a red trail on each cheek.

The ringing continued.

It must be the police—PC McGann and his men. They know what I've done. They're here to arrest me.

Her hands shook even more as she opened the front door.

"All right, Joycie?" It was Mr Reed. "I have some very important news."

Bounding inside, he barged right past her down the hallway.

"Come in," Joyce whispered, shutting the door.

"Took you a while to answer, didn't it?" he shouted from the living room.

When she caught up with him, he was sitting in her husband's favourite armchair.

"I was sleeping," she said.

"Well, you do need your beauty sleep," Reed smirked.

"Yes." She didn't like the way he was looking at her.

"I like your dress. What are those red splodges supposed to be? Berries?"

Joyce looked down at her blood-streaked dress. "Yes. Berries."

"May I touch the fabric?" His hand clawed towards her.

She jumped back. "I'd rather you didn't."

"No need to be shy around me, Joycie girl."

"You said . . . you said you had some news?"

"Oh, yes." Reed cleared his throat. "Any chance of a drink? I'm parched."

"I'm sorry. I have no drink."

"It doesn't have to be alcoholic, Joycie. Tea will do."

"No tea. No water. No drink."

"What? Not even water?"

"No. It's the taps, see. They've . . . gone all wrong."

"Oh?" Reed rose from the chair. "I'd best have a look at that for you."

"There's really no need . . ."

She scurried after him as he stormed into the kitchen.

"Dear oh dear. What's happened here?" He was standing over Olivia's broken jar. "Had a bit of an accident?"

"I dropped a jar."

"I can see that, Joycie. Where do you keep the dustpan and brush?"

"You don't have to . . ."

But he was already peering into cupboards and yanking at drawers. She noticed three long scratches running down his hand.

The black cat?

"You must have a dustpan and brush somewhere."

"No. Sorry. I'll . . ."

"No dustpan and brush? No water?" He eyed the empty gin bottles, the unwashed stack of plates in the sink. "I think you're telling me tales, Joycie girl. What's really going on?"

He stood, arms folded, by the washing machine. Joyce spied a wrinkled brown tentacle slithering out from behind it towards his legs. Leaping into action, she pulled him away.

"I'm sorry, Mr Reed. We're very busy today."

Out in the hallway, he looked down at the drops of blood on the carpet whilst Joyce opened the front door.

"Come back another time." Turning back, she saw him following the bloodstains up the stairs. "No, Mr Reed!"

Racing after him, her juddering legs were no match for his swift, curious stride. On reaching the landing, his shoes were already climbing the attic ladder.

As she collapsed, trembling, against the wall, she heard his voice call down from above:

"Well, well, well, Joycie girl. What do we have here?"

28. GRAVEYARD

Hunched in the rain, and tied to a pew, Beth trudged among the gravestones.

What the fuck just happened to me?

Had it all been a dream? She'd never even noticed a building in the graveyard before. Looking back, there was only a twisted thicket where it once stood.

It can't have been real.

But the old man was, wasn't he?

Something had to have tied me to this fucking pew.

He must have drugged her. She remembered an ammonia-like smell when his hands went over her mouth. She'd passed out and woken into . . .

. . . a nightmare.

It must have been a weird hallucination.

Why else would Marv appear and then vanish?

She thought she heard whispers from the downpour, murmurs beneath the soil. Ignoring them, she limped on, her movements hampered by the pew.

Jeez, this thing is killing my back.

Finally, she came to the low wall that ran alongside the gates.

Here goes.

Taking a run-up, she launched herself at the wall, backside first. Bouncing off, she landed in the mud, cursing—though the wood had splintered somewhat.

There's only one thing for it.

She got up and jumped again.

On her fourth attempt, the pew completely shattered, breaking away to the ground. With the wooden seat gone, her fabric bounds were looser; wriggling fiercely, she was able to pull them over her head.

Once free, she sat down on the rain-sodden wall, clutching her back and collecting her breath.

BEEP-BEEP! BEEP-BEEP!

Her heart leapt into her throat.

It's just my phone.

"Hello," she answered. "Oh, hi Mum . . . Yeah . . . I was at Darren's last night . . . No, I'm not working today . . . Sorry to make you worry . . . Yeah, I'm coming home now."

29. TEARS

Rain fell from the ashen sky, as tears fell from Joyce's eyes. She sat, crumpled, on her living room sofa with Mr Reed.

"It's all right, Joycie. It's all right."

"But . . . I didn't . . . I loved . . . ohh."

"I know, I know." Reed placed his hand on her knee. "But why did you do it? I mean, he was all right, wasn't he?"

"Yes," Joyce sniffed. "I loved him."

"Then *why*?"

Looking within herself, she found only a long black cloud. "Well, he did like trains."

"I suppose that *is* a bit weird," said Reed. "Still, I never saw your husband as much of a threat. You obviously did."

Joyce let out a harsh sob, burying her head in her hands.

"Look," said Reed. "If it makes you feel any better, I killed someone yesterday."

Joyce lifted her head. "I know. The boy on the war monument."

Reed shook his head. "That was a mercy killing on behalf of the town. We all took part. No, I'm talking about a solo mission. I killed Eric."

Joyce looked aghast. "The old feller who always eats sweets? The one whose wife died?"

"That's the one," said Reed.

"But why?"

"The same reason the town decides to kill someone. I just took it upon myself to act alone. Just like you did with your husband."

Joyce cleared her throat. "But I thought Eric was harmless."

"Oh, dear God, no," said Reed. "Just before I slit his throat, I caught him listening to sad, weird music. It was very odd. Wouldn't be surprised if it was linked to witchcraft in some way. And besides, he had a black cat."

Joyce gasped. Reed continued:

"I thought it could be the one you were looking for. Especially as I'd noticed the old man talking to it whenever I broke into his house. He was definitely some sort of weirdo. After I killed him, I stole his cat. I have it at home, along with several others. That's why I called round in the first place. I want you to inspect them, Joyce. See if I've got the right one."

"I see," said Joyce.

"But first," Reed leapt to his feet, "we must get rid of the evidence. Just in case the town decides that your husband wasn't a weirdo after all, and you killed him for no good reason. You would be in a lot of trouble then."

"You're not going to tell anyone, are you?" she stammered.

"Don't worry about that, Joycie girl," he winked. "It's much better for me if your husband is dead, anyway."

"Oh."

"So," he slapped his hands together loudly. "Do you have an axe?"

"In . . . In the pantry."

"Righto! And later I'll need a bucket and mop with some hot water and bleach."

"What are you . . .?"

"Ha ha. Don't worry, Joycie. I know your taps are working, really. Don't think I believed all that crap you gave me earlier about having no water."

"No."

"You were just scared and wanted me to leave, that's all."

"Yes."

He patted her head. "Good girl. Now, you just sit tight, and I'll take care of everything."

Moments later, she could hear him up in the attic, chopping her dead husband into pieces with an axe.

"You know, Joycie," he called down from above, "I think you and I are the only ones in this town who aren't fucking crazy."

30. BENNY & DARREN

"Morning!"

Benny and Darren both opened their eyes at the same time. They were lying on the garage floor, wrapped in each other's arms.

"Shit," said Darren, looking for his jeans.

"Fuck," said Benny, pulling up his tracksuit bottoms.

Luckily, they were hidden behind a rusting chassis when Darren's father, Mr Thompson, came down from upstairs.

"Are you in here, boys?"

Darren's head bobbed up from behind the old car. "Alright, Dad?"

"There you are, son. Sorry, I overslept. It was some night last night, eh?"

"Yeah," said Darren, smiling down at Benny. "Sure was."

"Is Benny in yet?"

"Here I am, Mr Thompson." Benny's head popped up beside Darren's.

"Good of you both to get straight to work on the chassis. I didn't think you'd be in today—what with the way you were carrying on last night."

"What do you mean?" asked Benny.

Mr Thompson's moustache quivered. "Well, the way you were putting it back . . . You must have pretty sore heads this morning. I know I do. And I left early."

It was true. Both young men felt as though someone had hammered nails through their brains.

"What time did you lads leave, anyway?"

"Can't remember," said Darren.

"Must have been a good night then," his father chuckled, before suddenly clutching his head. "Fuck me. I feel rough as a bear's arse. You lads keep working on that motor. I'm just popping into town for some paracetamol. Do you want anything from the shops?"

"No thanks," said Darren.

"Yeah," said Benny. "Just get us some cans of pop and a couple of bacon sandwiches."

"Cheeky fuckers," Mr Thompson fumed. "I'm not made of money. Get your own sodding pop and sarnies."

With that, he stormed out.

Darren waited a while before hissing at his friend: "He almost fucking caught us."

Benny shrugged. "He's going to have to find out sometime."

"He'd kill us."

"The whole town would kill us."

Darren knew it was true. He wandered over to the workbench and toyed with a spanner. Then he pulled out his phone. "I'm going to call Beth."

"Why?" Benny snorted. "She doesn't give a fuck about you."

"I just need to speak to her. That's all."

"Are you going to tell her about us?"

"Maybe." Darren called her number.

"Bitch probably won't pick it up anyway," said Benny. "She never answered all the times you were ringing last night."

"I hope she's ok," said Darren.

"I hope she's dead," said Benny.

"Shh." To Darren's surprise, Beth answered. She sounded worse than he felt himself. "Where the fuck were you last night?" he spat. "What? . . . Really?" He looked over at Benny, then walked into the office for privacy. "Are you serious?"

Benny rolled his eyes and stepped over to the workbench, where he pretended to engage with some tools. It was a while before Darren came out and stood behind him.

"Well?" Benny crossed his arms. "What did she say?"

Darren exhaled. "She said that she was kidnapped last night. She was taken to a weird building in the graveyard and tied to some kind of bench. When she woke up, there was a crazy old man, spouting shit. A giant cross fell down and stabbed him. The whole building caved in. But she saw Marv, who helped her escape. And the building vanished."

Benny howled with laughter. "Yeah, right. You must be fucking stupid to believe all that."

Darren shook his head. "I didn't tell her Marv is dead. She sounded pretty scared. She's at home now. Said she was gonna sleep for the rest of the day."

"Sounds like she's gone fucking mad. I always knew she was a weirdo."

"She told me not to tell anyone."

Benny turned to his friend and grinned. "I wonder what the town would make of her crazy story. They don't like weirdoes here."

"You wouldn't."

"I would." Benny rubbed his hand over Darren's crotch. "Anything to keep them away from us."

31. KITCHEN

"There you go, Joycie: Another river suicide."

Mr Reed came downstairs clutching a bulging black bin liner, which he threw at Joyce's feet. She was sitting at the kitchen table now, drinking gin.

"Mr Reed, my husband wouldn't have committed suicide by chopping himself up with an axe. It wasn't his style."

Reed shrugged, helping himself to her booze. "What you need is a good drink."

Her pale, shaking hands clutched a mug to her blood-smeared breast. "I've already had a good drink. And it isn't doing any good."

He put his hand on her shoulder. "Let's go down to the pub; enjoy ourselves for once."

"But my hair . . ." Joyce gestured towards the wiry, grey nest erupting from her scalp; split ends encrusted with her husband's drying blood.

"Looks fine to me," said Reed.

"I've nothing to wear."

"You look beautiful, Joyce." His eyes ran up and down her body. "Let's go out and knock 'em dead."

She knocked his hand off her shoulder and walked to the sink. Slumping over, she eyed her jowls reflected in the tap. "I feel so old," she groaned.

He bounded up behind her, planting a hard wet kiss on the side of her face and grabbing her hips. "Neither of us are getting any younger, Joycie."

Behind them, the bin liner on the floor started to twitch.

32. LIFE

Bloody fingers wormed their way through a rip in the black plastic, followed by a whole hand. Sliding out to the kitchen floor, it crawled forth like a fleshy spider, pulling itself along by its fingers, dragging a tail of snapped bones and torn tendons.

From behind the washing machine, an oily black eye watched the hand make its way towards the sink, where Joyce struggled in Mr Reed's arms.

"Come on, Joycie. You know you want it."

"Not now, please."

She pushed him back hard against the table. "You're all the same," he huffed, pouring himself a gin.

Joyce continued to lament her ageing reflection in the taps.

With a groaning wheeze, Olivia un-suckered herself from the back of the washing machine and squelched out to follow the hand, her tentacles slapping on the lino.

Joyce thought the sound was Reed gulping gin; Reed thought Joyce's nervous stomach was getting the better of her.

The hand paused by Reed's shoes. Grasping the fabric of his trousers, it began to pull itself up.

Sulking, Reed poured more gin.

The hand climbed his leg, nestling round his crotch.

Reed put down his glass. "Why, Joycie," he leered. "I knew you wanted me, really."

Joyce spun round from the sink, looking puzzled. And then she screamed.

Her dead husband's fingers clamped down on Reed's testicles. It was his turn to scream.

"Get off me! Get off me!" Beating at the disembodied hand with a gin bottle, Reed only succeeded in bashing his balls.

Below, another hand scuttled out through the ripped bin liner, dragging itself across the floor like a bony crab. Finding purchase in the folds of Joyce's blood-soaked dress, it fingered its way up her body.

But Joyce was distracted by something else.

"Olivia!" she cried.

Her child shuffled towards her through broken glass.

"What the fuck is that?" Reed yelled, still slamming the bottle against his groin.

"Your daughter," Joyce blurted.

"What?"

Olivia opened her slimy jaws, showing Mummy and Daddy her teeth.

Reed turned and vomited against the wall. Joyce couldn't stop screaming. Then she finally noticed the other hand: Her husband's fingers were now prying through the flabby flesh of her throat, looking for something to throttle.

Backed against the cabinet, Joyce groped at the drawers. Yanking one open, amid a clatter of cutlery, she pulled out a kitchen knife and slashed wildly. With a sickening *phut*, the blade sunk into the creeping hand. It thudded to the lino, the knife still embedded in its back.

Joyce looked down, rubbing her neck. When the hand didn't move, she let out a relieved breath.

Then the fingers twitched, drumming an off-beat rhythm, as it clawed its way up her dress again.

"Get away from me!"

At Reed's feet, the bin liner writhed. Arthur's head rolled out through the rips, looking like a ball of red mincemeat. Wobbling to a stop by Reed's shoes, one sad grey eye stared up through the pulp.

"Oh, fuck off!" Reed grumped. "I'm still trying to get your hand off my cock!"

A raw scarlet mush, the head raised itself from the floor, teetering on the entrails of its severed neck.

"Piss off!" Reed flung the gin bottle. It bounced off Arthur's head and smashed against the pantry door.

"Shit."

A black hole gaped in the ruins of Arthur's face; it was full of gnashing teeth. They tried to sink themselves into Reed's footwear.

"Oh no, mate. Not my new Hush Puppies." Swinging his leg, Reed booted the head. It went sailing through the air, entrails dangling, and crashed against the window, shattering the glass.

With a great gasp, Joyce finally wrenched her husband's other hand from her throat. She hurled it out through the broken window after the head. On hearing it land in the weeds outside, she jumped over her mewling daughter and tugged at the hand on Reed's balls.

"Careful!" he winced.

"It won't let go," Joyce cried. "It's attached itself like a bloody limpet!"

She went back to her drawers and returned with a hammer.

"Steady, Joyce," Reed gulped. "Steady."

Raising the hammer, she swatted at the hand with leaden swings. "Stand still, Mr Reed!"

"I'm trying!"

Boof!

She hit the hand, square on. It dropped to the floor and scurried away.

Reed fell against the table, breathing hard. Joyce thought he looked pale.

"Well, that seemed to do the trick," she said, tossing the hammer over her shoulder. It smashed something on touchdown, but she didn't care.

"Let's get out of here." Reed eyed Olivia's slithery, raised tentacles. "Quickly!"

Grabbing Joyce's arm, he ran for the front door. Out in the rain, he dragged her towards his parked car. "My wife's at home so you can sit in the front with me."

As Reed started the engine and raced off, two crawling hands, a wobbling head, and a little one-eyed mutant with six legs followed them down the road.

33. TRUE

"See you at the pub at eight?"

Benny wiped his hands on an oily rag. It was five o'clock and he had downed tools.

"Yeah," said Darren. "See you then."

Benny kissed him gently on the corner of his mouth.

It was all right. No one was looking.

Sliding the garage doors closed, Darren watched Benny walk away down the road.

Before going to the pub, there was something he had to do.

When Benny was out of sight, Darren began the short walk to the graveyard. On finding the cemetery gates chained shut, he vaulted over a low wall, landing on some shattered bits of wood and old rags. Kicking them aside, he sauntered onwards through the rain and mud, shivering in his coveralls.

Only a pussy would wear a coat.

Passing overturned gravestones and graffitied tombs, he came to the bramble bush.

This is where she said it happened.

Crouching down, he could see nothing unusual. But, stepping round to the other side, he found a pile of bricks, with a wooden beam protruding from their centre, like some makeshift grave.

Darren pulled some of the stones away, revealing a bearded face, twisted into a scream beneath a crown of thorns.

Shit.

Stepping back, he realised that it was a plaster effigy pinned to a cross. He scraped more bricks away, until he touched something chilly: Two bony white hands clasped the base of the cross, congealing globs of blood welling up between the long fingers.

Fuck.

After rubbing his own hands down his legs, Darren pulled out his phone. It was a while before the voice he needed to hear answered.

"Beth? . . . It's Darren . . . I know you're trying to sleep . . . Listen . . . I'm in the graveyard . . . I've found the cross and a load of old bricks . . . Of course I believed you! . . . Yeah, looks like it's stuck in someone's stomach. There's lots of blood . . . The old man, yeah . . . I can see his fucking hands . . . Listen . . . What you said . . . it's true . . . Meet me at the pub in three hours . . . Something's going on here . . . We need to talk . . . Okay, yeah, I'll see you then . . . Love you . . . Bye."

As Darren shoved the phone back in his pocket, he saw a familiar stooped figure at the opposite end of the cemetery.

No.

It was standing by the ferns that led to the river.

It can't be . . .

But there was no mistaking the sodden duffle coat and dark tangle of hair.

She was right.

Through falling sheets of rain, Darren moved closer, until he could see the puffed purple face and bulging eyelids. One of them opened with an audible *rip*; a veiny yellow eye glared out. Torn lips drew back over broken teeth. A lumpy, freezing hand reached out.

And all Darren could hear was the snap of bones.

34. HOME

Having driven through the empty wet streets in silence, Reed stopped the car before a row of terraced houses on the outskirts of town.

"Home sweet home," he said, turning to Joyce.

She continued to stare ahead, hands tremoring in her lap.

"Come on, love."

He dragged her out of the car and through a squeaking gateway, into his house.

"Upstairs!" he commanded. Once they'd climbed the creaking staircase to the landing, he pushed her into his bedroom and shut the door behind them.

Joyce sat down on the edge of the bed, facing the wardrobe.

"It's all right." Reed was peeping out through the curtained window. "There's no sign of them."

Joyce looked down to her trembling hands. She was still trying to make sense of all that had just happened.

Reed plonked himself down beside her. "We'd best stay here until the coast is clear."

Joyce nodded slowly.

"Say, Joycie. Did you say that thing was my daughter?"

"It . . . She might be," Joyce whispered. "Her name is Olivia."

"Well, blow me down," Reed slapped his thigh. "I always wanted to have children, but my wife . . . she's disabled. This calls for a celebration! I've got some tins of ale somewhere."

"No, it's all right, Mr Reed. I don't want to drink anymore."

Reed pretended not to hear, as he pulled up heaps of old clothes, searching for the booze. "You managed to keep it a secret long enough, didn't you, Joycie? Why'd you never tell me I was a father?"

"I thought you'd be ashamed. Olivia isn't normal, after all."

"She looks disgusting," Reed agreed. "Made me sick when I saw her."

"It's the cat's fault," Joyce explained. "It took her soul, made her a monster."

Reed slapped his forehead. "How could I forget? That cat! I have it in my wardrobe."

He bounded over to the wardrobe and pulled open its doors. A rotten, fishy stench hit Joyce's nose as she rose to take a look. Inside, 13 lifeless black cats stood upright on the shelves.

Joyce covered her nose with shaking fingers.

"You admire my work?" Reed smiled. "I practice the art of taxidermy in my spare time. I am a dab hand with the old needle and thread. I have captured these slaves to Evil and preserved their bodies for all to see. What do you think? Can you see the cat?"

Joyce shook her head. "No. I don't see the cat that took Olivia's soul." She slumped back down on the bed. "It's all so hopeless, Mr Reed."

"Hey, don't speak like that." He squeezed her shoulder. "We'll find the cat one day. Then we'll cut it open and retrieve Olivia's soul. Then we'll put it back in Olivia and she'll be normal. Then we'll be happy." He kissed her cheek.

Tears began to stream from her eyes. "She was conceived the night of the dance. Do you remember?"

"I'll never forget," Reed grinned. "How's about we go for round two?"

Shoving her down, his hands tugged frantically at the blood-encrusted buttons of her dress.

"No, Mr Reed. No!" As she squirmed beneath him, her head hit a bump in the bed. "Urgh. What's that?"

Reed stopped fumbling. "Oh, yes: Joyce, meet my wife."

From her uncomfortable, prone position, Joyce craned her neck back and saw the shape of a woman lying beneath the covers.

"Good grief, Mr Reed!"

Raising her knees into his stomach, she pushed him away and rolled onto her feet.

"I'm awfully sorry, Mrs Reed," she bowed before the body on the mattress.

"There's no need for that," wheezed Reed, rubbing his belly. "My wife is disabled. She's deaf and dumb and can't walk."

"I know that," said Joyce. "I just didn't know she was in here with us."

"She won't mind. She doesn't know what's going on. She's completely useless."

"How can you speak about your wife like that?"

"It's true."

"I think I should leave."

"What about your husband? He's out there somewhere . . . in bits. And he wants to kill us."

"It's a chance I have to take."

She made for the door, but Reed blocked her way. "You're not going anywhere, Joyce. You're staying here with me."

35. MAD

"Mr Reed, you're mad!"

Joyce stepped back towards the bed. Reed still blocked the door.

"Yes, I'm mad," he cried. "Mad with love for you!"

"But . . . your wife—"

"Forget her. She's disabled."

"Mr Reed! Your wife does not deserve this. I am taking her with me, and we are leaving right now. I won't allow her to be trapped in this house with you any longer. You're insane."

Joyce yanked back the bedcovers and screamed. A thing of rags lay on the mattress; its black button eyes staring up at her.

"What the hell is this?" Joyce shrieked.

"My wife," said Reed, stepping slowly towards her. "I made her myself. I told you I'm a dab hand with the old needle and thread."

"You said your wife was disabled. We all believed you."

"She is," said Reed. "She's deaf and dumb and cannot walk."

"She's made of cloth, you fool!"

With that, Joyce grabbed the lightweight, raggedy doll and hurled it at his head.

"Uuurrgh!"

He fell back against the wardrobe, knocking the doors open. Thirteen screeching black cats leapt free in a furry blur, pushing him to the floor. Their sawdust-filled legs moved with stiff, swift jerks.

Pulling his wife from his face, Reed stared, aghast, as the hissing creatures swarmed over him, all fangs, claws and flashing eyes.

"Be gone, you little devils! Be gone!"

Joyce ran for the door. Glancing back, she saw the once-dead cats bite down into Reed's screaming face, leaving it as red and ragged as a hunk of raw meat.

Bile rose in her throat. Gulping, she rushed downstairs to the front door. It was locked.

"Where's the key?"

Paws padded on the stairs. Looking up, she saw the cats descending, shreds of bloodied flesh hanging from their mouths.

"Shit!"

Joyce raced through the nearest door, slamming it shut behind her. The room was dark and musty. Fumbling along the wall, she flicked a switch and light filled the room. She gasped. The walls were covered in pictures of her: There she was from afar, walking to the off-licence, or on her way to work. And there she was, in unforgiving close-up, tucked up in bed, next to Arthur.

A shiver ran down her back.

The rest of the room was full of clutter. Piles of old dresses and pornographic magazines littered the floor. She waded her way through them to the heavily curtained window. Pulling back the greenish-brown drapes, she heard scratches at the door. It creaked open. Black furry heads poked through; green eyes glinting; red mouths growling.

"Get away from me!" Joyce whimpered. "Leave me alone!"

She looked around for something to smash the window with. Her eyes fell upon a nude figurine on the mantlepiece. Reaching for it, she noticed that a photograph of her own face had been crudely glued to the statuette's.

How tasteless.

A cat leapt up and scratched her hand, tearing the shame from her mind.

"Get away!"

She swung the figurine at the beasts by her feet, then turned to the window. Using all her fear and anger, she smashed the statuette against the panes. As glass exploded, claws scraped down the backs of her legs.

"You little bastards are ruining my tights!"

Wincing against the pain, she threw the figurine at their heads, then heaved herself up onto the sill, her hands crunching through broken glass.

Diving through the shattered panes, she landed on the garden path and lurched to the gate on twisted ankles.

The cats soared after her.

"Oh, fuck."

Opening the gate, she was greeted by an unwelcome sight: Waiting on the pavement was a wobbling head and two scuttling hands.

"I'm sorry, Arthur," she screamed. "Please make this stop!"

But all she heard in answer was a squelching from above. Gazing upwards, she saw Olivia unstick herself from a tree. Sailing down through the air, tentacles flailing, she landed with a sloppy thud on Joyce's face. Wrapping her veiny brown limbs round Mama's head, the mutant child gurgled with delight. Joyce, meanwhile, choked and gagged on her daughter's slimy, wrinkled skin.

Although blinded by the pulsing blob suckered to her face, Joyce tore off down the road as fast as she could. And two scampering hands, a ripped-up head, and 13 dead black cats chased after her.

36. TONY'S LAST DANCE

Tony put on an old record. It was one of those songs that made you feel like you were in love, even when you weren't.

In his mind, he danced through the Grotto with Beryl Flynn, the forgotten Hollywood glamour-girl. She had the finest pair of cheekbones he'd ever seen, and the loveliest pair of eyes. Nice hair, too.

Careering round the empty shop, she slipped inside his arms so well.

"Oh, Tony," she giggled. "I also have a large record collection. But it's not as big as yours. Do you like the Small Faces? Oh, you do? They're my favourite band. Would you like to come back to mine and listen to my new, remastered edition of *Ogdens' Nut Gone Flake*?"

"Oh, I'd love to, Beryl. I really would. I . . ."

Tony's voice sounded flat and hollow in the empty shop. His arms were empty, too. He stood alone, sweaty and out of breath.

The record had finished. As he lifted it from the turntable, Joyce Burke went hurtling past the window behind him. With Olivia wrapped round her head, she was still being chased by two crawling hands, a decapitated head, and 13 mewling cats.

What's that noise?

Tony's heart juddered on hearing the cats. He still had nightmares about the beast that tore out his eye.

Fingering the glass replacement, he walked to the window and peered out. There was nothing there. Only the neon-lit darkness and rain-slicked streets.

He put the record back in its sleeve and filed it away.

"If only I were made of plastic," he sighed, stuffing his hands in his pockets. He pulled out fluff and loose change. There was enough money there for a beer, or two. He sniffed his arm pits and winced.

Squeezing into a new shirt, he looked up to the face of Jonas Koop, staring down from his photo on the wall.

"Forgive me, Mr Koop. I have to go back to that place where they . . . It's the only place I might find . . . All I've ever wanted is a girl in my arms."

The little bell tinkled as Tony opened the door and stepped out.

At least it's stopped raining.

He pulled the rattling door shut, and silence fell over the shop once more.

37. THE PUB

The Fox & Newt pub stood alongside a dark stretch of river, half-concealed by bushes. As Beth approached the doors, her stomach fluttered. She no longer felt safe.

The walk down had been an ordeal: jumping at every drunken howl and animal cry. But she had to see Darren one final time. Tell him it was over. She owed him that much; they'd been through a lot together. She may have once loved him, but she realised now that she'd never really *liked* him.

Reaching for the doorhandle, she heard something crash through the shrubbery behind her. Looking back, she saw a woman in a bedraggled dress, staggering forwards, arms outstretched, with what looked like a jellyfish wrapped round her head.

"Fucking pissheads," Beth muttered, once the initial shock had passed.

She watched the woman stumble towards the river, then turned back to the pub entrance. She did not see the scampering hands and disembodied head, or the 13 cats that followed. Nor did she hear the splash from the river as they vanished within the water's depths: Woman, jelly-creature and all.

Taking a deep breath, Beth pushed open the doors. A crowd of faces glowered back at her from above their foaming pints. There were about 30 men packed inside the dimly lit tavern: every one of them familiar. But the most recognisable male lay across the central table, pale and dripping wet.

"Darren!" She froze in the doorway.

"Aye, it's Darren." Benny stood by her lover's body, wearing his best tracksuit. His face was fixed and stern. "Old Malc found him by the river. His skull's been caved in."

Old Malc, the pub landlord, sat in the corner with his arm round Darren's father. Mr Thompson's head was buried in his hands.

Beth rushed over to him, but Benny raised his palm.

"She's the one who did this," he yelled.

"No," Beth cried. "I'd never—"

"Everyone knows you and Darren weren't getting along. So, you decided to get rid of him."

"That's not true—"

"So, you weren't arguing?"

"Well, yes, but—"

"A liar as well as a murderer," Benny went on. "She's also mad. She sees things which aren't there."

"No!"

"Why don't you tell us about the crazy old man in the graveyard, and the imaginary building he took you to, which then fell down?"

Beth fell silent.

Everyone squirmed, then looked to Darren's father. The old man lifted his tear-streaked face. "She killed my son," he nodded. "We must kill her."

38. BURN

The tavern regulars rose from their seats, eyes glaring. They trudged towards Beth, slowly at first. And then they let out a roar.

Beth turned away, screaming, as they began to charge. Tripping through the doors, she ran towards the moonlit river. The townsfolk heaved after her, waving their fists and shouting: "Kill! Kill!"

Among the 30 shrieking faces was the butcher, the chemist, the baker, the bank manager—and Tony, the music shop owner, who straggled at the back, looking sheepish.

"Grab a stick, lads," said PC McGann, who was off duty that night. "Set it on fire. Let's burn the witch!"

Running to the riverbank, they gathered snapped branches and set them alight. Holding the flaming sticks aloft, they charged after the dark-haired girl in the parka. Some of the men had to stop every so often and bring up mucus. Beth heard them retching behind her.

Wincing with disgust, she suddenly slipped, jerking through the mud. Stumbling sideways, she crashed down the muddy bank, just below the bridge, rolling to a stop before the river's edge. Pain shot through her back and she clenched her eyes.

On opening them, she saw flaming torches bobbing in the dark above, and twisted faces leering down beneath the trees. They were so close now that she could feel the heat from the flames.

"We have you now, you little bitch."

Benny made his way to the front of the crowd, and lowered his torch to her face.

39. MOB

"Wait!"

A voice sounded from the back of the crowd.

"Wait," it said again, growing closer.

The ugly mob parted to let the hinderer through, raising their torches to light his face. It was Tony. He was out of breath by the time he'd pushed his way to the front.

"What do you want?" Mr Thompson growled.

"Just give me a minute," Tony wheezed, dropping his torch to the ground. They looked at him, rapt, as he stood bent over, hands on knees, sweat dripping from his head. He was totally unused to any form of exercise, let alone running along a riverbank and holding a burning stick in the air.

He felt the eyes of the crowd sear into him. He didn't like being the centre of attention; he preferred to remain invisible, hence his position at the back of the crowd.

Finally, he spoke. "How do you know this girl is responsible for the young lad's death?"

"Because I said so," sneered Benny.

The others hooted in agreement. Beth lay curled in the dirt, silently weeping.

"But how do you know?" Tony repeated.

Benny merely laughed. "Out of our way, fatty."

But Tony didn't move. He stood before the girl, shielding her with his girth.

Benny picked up Tony's dropped torch and turned to the mob. "There's only one thing for it, lads. Burn the fat bastard!"

The mob cheered in approval and moved forward, shouting: "Burn! Burn!"

Tony felt his bowels loosen, but though his instincts screamed at him to run, he refused: He remembered Jonas Koop, and he couldn't let it happen again.

"Burn! Burn!"

Some of these scowling faces were there the night Koop died. Some of these people were responsible.

Tony backed away. The flames from the nearest torch singed the hairs in his nose. Slipping into the river, he stumbled, swaying for balance. The mob laughed and continued to surge forward; the orange glow of their torches reflected on the water's surface.

"Burn! Burn!"

Tony kept moving back, until the freezing currents were up to his knees.

Lunging through the water after him, Benny thrust both of his torches into Tony's gut.

The record shop owner howled as the flames lit his shirt. For an instant, he was shocked into paralysis, so intense was the burning pain.

Whimpering, he fell back into the freezing water, thrashing about until the flames were doused. He emerged, panting, moments later, amid a black stinking smog. His shirt fell away in blackened rags, exposing his red, burnt stomach. The frigid air was, for once, a blessing.

Benny swung his torches again, teeth clenched. Tony dodged the flames. Benny kept lashing out, and the rest of the mob followed him further into the water.

"Burn! Burn!"

"Leave him alone."

The mob turned, gasping.

Beth stood on the riverbank, her voice shaky but firm. "You have to stop. Please, listen to me—"

"Silence, witch," Mr Thompson glowered. "You killed my son."

"No, Mr Thompson. I would never—"

But her voice was drowned out by an almighty cry of: "Burn her!"

Ignoring Tony, they began to move in her direction.

Beth tried to run, but her feet had sunk into the mud.

PC McGann was at the front of the crowd this time, with Benny taking up the rear. Further back, Tony squatted underwater, soothing his hot, scarred belly in the cool depths. He waited until there was enough distance between him and the others, before he started doggy-paddling to the other side. All the way across, he heard their cries rend the air.

"Burn her! Burn the witch!"

40. THE RIVER

Charging through the water, PC McGann was much further ahead than the rest of the men.

"I'm going to burn you, you little witch!"

He was close enough now that Beth could see the saliva frothing in his mouth.

Suddenly, he tripped, and Beth finally plucked her feet from the mud, almost losing a trainer in the process. Scrambling up the muddy bank, she heard the policeman scream behind her: "What the fuck was that?"

McGann looked down and saw something stare back at him through the filthy water. Then, with a splash, it reached up and grabbed his face.

The clutching hand was followed by a thin white arm and a bald, bloated head with bulging eyes. Then the rest of the body emerged: a sagging bag of purpling flesh with a large, bloody rip in its chest. As McGann tried to free himself from the creature's grasp, he felt skin flake off beneath his nails.

The rest of the mob was a little further back. They froze as McGann grappled with the thing in the water, keeping as still and silent as they would before a venomous snake.

"That's Joe Cummings," Old Malc gasped. "We killed him last month."

"You mean the 'river suicide'?" said Mr Thompson.

Malc nodded.

They stood, waist-deep in the river, watching as Joe grasped McGann's face with bony claws.

Suddenly, they heard a *pop*, and McGann stumbled back, rubbing his scalp. Lowering his hand, he gaped at the white, blood-flecked shards on his fingertips. Gummy lumps of brain slid down his face and hit the river's surface.

Joe scooped the fatty tissue up to his lips.

McGann tried to piece his head back together. But the broken bits of bone just fell through the holes. Letting out a dull groan, his eyes rolled back, and he sank beneath the surface.

"Shit," Mr Thompson hissed. "What are we going to do?"

In response, Benny hurled one of his torches at the monster's head. It bounced off into the water, sizzling out with a *hiss*. Joe glared back at them, his mouldy teeth gnawing through McGann's brain.

"For fuck's sake, burn it!" Benny yowled, thrashing forward. The others followed, holding their torches high.

As they started to move, ripples broke out across the surface. And more and more bodies began to rise all around them. Each one was grey and crusty with striking red wounds.

Benny tried to count them. Ten. Twelve. Fifteen . . .

A headless thing in a leather jacket staggered towards him, water cascading from its arms. Benny swung his remaining torch, keeping it at bay.

Another thing sprang up and sunk its teeth into Malc's cheek. The old man hollered as his blood sprayed into the river.

The other "suicides" glared at the spurting, crimson fluid, licking their chapped lips with swollen black tongues.

Noting this diversion, Benny sprang into action. "Run!" he shouted.

The crowd clumped back towards dry land, swinging their torches. Although some of the revenants caught fire, this didn't stop them lunging. Their charred fingers kept grasping and their scorched jaws gnashed.

"Christ on a bicycle!" Mr Thompson screamed. "Why won't they die?"

Benny spat into the river. "Because they're already dead."

41. THE HILL

Having climbed the muddy riverbank, Beth was now ascending the grassy hill that led to the road. Midway up, she glanced behind and saw three or four men racing after her, drenched and angry, with torches aloft.

"There she is! Get her!"

Others clambered onto the riverbank, pursued by burning cadavers. Mr Thompson was wrestling with one such entity at the river's edge.

Beth kept on running. On finally reaching the pavement at the top, she saw Tony leaning against the bus stop, soaked and out of breath.

"Thank you," she said, walking over to him.

"Yup," Tony panted.

Beth eyed the nasty-looking burns that criss-crossed his torso. "You need to get that seen to."

He nodded. "I have some bandages at home."

"Got you now, witch!"

Beth spun around as Benny came over the crest of the hill, followed by a gaggle of men.

"I thought you'd been eaten," Benny sneered at Tony.

Suddenly, Benny's face lit up like a Halloween pumpkin in the glare of oncoming lamps.

Tony flagged down the oncoming bus. As the doors hissed open, he pushed Beth aboard, then hopped on behind. Benny bounded after them, but the doors swished shut on his foot.

"No burning sticks allowed," said the driver, pulling away from the kerb.

As the bus sped off into town, the diminished mob stood slouched on the pavement. There were seven of them left now. Benny stared down at the corpses littering the hill. His former drinking buddies were being guzzled by flaming ghouls.

"She is responsible for this." Benny turned back to his remaining friends. "She brought them back to life with her witchcraft, and she's ordered them to kill us. We must gather more forces and get her to remove the curse. Then we must destroy her."

The others nodded in agreement. Worn-out but determined, they stalked off in the direction of town, their torches staining the darkness red.

42. RITUAL

The bus pulled up outside the Grotto and Tony and Beth jumped out. The short journey had been endured in confused, exhausted silence, but now it was time for action.

Inside the shop, Beth ordered Tony to take a cool shower whilst she acquainted herself with his first aid kit. When he came back down, she laid him on the counter and began dressing his wounds.

"What the hell is going on?"

Tony winced as she bandaged his stomach. "It's the dead, innit. They're coming back to life."

"That's impossible . . ."

"Well, that's what's happening. All those people they killed . . ."

"Who killed?"

"The town."

"What do you mean?"

"Don't you know? The 'river suicides'? They didn't kill themselves. They were murdered. Cheers, love."

Beth had finished bandaging Tony. He slid down from the counter and put on a fresh T-shirt.

"Ritual murder," he continued. "They were killed because they were different. They didn't fit in. It's the town's idea of keeping order. They've been doing it for years. You must have noticed?"

Beth shook her head, stunned.

"Your boyfriend was one of the ringleaders."

"Somebody killed him."

"I'll bet it was one of his victims."

Beth leaned against the counter, grasping her head. "The crazy old man in the graveyard . . . he kept going on about atonement. 'The day of atonement is here'. He said that the town was a snake or something. That it would turn around and bite us all . . ."

"Sounds about right," said Tony. "Feel free to take a shower, love. I have some clean clothes, but they might be a bit big for you."

Beth looked down at her muddy parka. "It's all right. I'm still struggling to get my head round all this."

"Speaking of heads," said Tony, "have you heard of Jonas Koop?"

"Yeah. I love his music."

"They cut off his head, you know? I was there the night they killed him. He was one of the town's first victims."

"I thought he went missing . . . about 30 years ago." Beth sank down onto a pile of books.

"Yeah, this has been going on so long." Tony slouched. "I've known, and I've done nothing about it."

"But you helped me tonight," said Beth. "Why'd you wait until now to stand up to them?"

"Because I always knew I could be next." Tony gestured towards the colourful items filling his shop. "No one with a passion for anything, other than what they approve of, is allowed to live. To them, it's weird; odd. Emotion scares them."

Beth nodded. "Darren was like that."

"That's why they killed Koop; his music was full of feeling they didn't understand." Tony's glass eye misted over. "I gave up a good career as an accountant to open this place. To them, that's not normal. Even my own mother never forgave me. All they care about is money. But I've been happier without it." He shook his head. "I thought that if I just kept quiet, kept going to the pub, they'd leave me alone. As long as I kept up the pretence of being normal . . ."

"What's normal?" Beth interjected. "Staying silent while others die?"

"I know I'm just as bad as them for doing nothing," said Tony, "but all I wanted was to be accepted; to fit in."

Beth stared at the floor, thinking of the days she avoided Marv whilst seeing Darren. "Me too," she shrugged. "But what can we do now?"

"I don't know," said Tony. "I'm sorry."

"Don't be."

"I am," Tony murmured. "You see, I did a bad thing and . . . well, all this might be my fault."

43. THE BOOK

"What do you mean?" asked Beth.

Tony walked into a back room. "Wait here. I'll show you."

He emerged moments later, clutching a dusty hardback book with no cover or title.

"What's that?"

"It belonged to that Marv kid. I saw your boyfriend and his mate take it off him and throw it into the hotel shrubbery, the night of the end-of-school dance . . ."

Beth sighed. "Darren used to bully Marv quite a lot . . . God, he was such a prick. I should never have stayed with him. He beat Marv up yesterday, made everyone join in. Thankfully, he got away . . ."

"No, love. They killed him."

"But I saw him in the graveyard. Or at least I think I did."

"He must have come back."

"Shit." Beth pulled out her wallet and removed a small scrap of paper. "He wrote me this poem. I always loved Marv's poems. They made me feel special."

"Words have power," Tony agreed. "Especially those in the boy's book. I went to get it back for him once the coast was clear, but he'd disappeared inside a hedge."

"Huh?"

"Your boyfriend pushed him through . . . anyway, what matters is that I decided to keep the book here at the shop, as the boy was a regular customer, and I could return it later. However, I became so engrossed that I just had to hold onto it. You see, it's an ancient magic book, full of incantations. The first one I noticed was a love spell. I decided to try it."

Beth put the poem back in her wallet. "Did it work?"

"Well, no . . . but then I found a spell for raising the dead. And I wanted to see if I could bring Koop back. Think of it: I could produce new records for Koop and we'd both be famous! According to the book, all I had to do was arrange the number 27 in a ritualistic pattern around my home. So, I repriced all my stock . . ."

"Why 27?"

"The book said it's *the* sacred number. And I agree. All the greats died at 27; I was that age when I lost my eye; and Koop died 27 years ago . . ."

"It's just coincidence, surely?"

"Coincidence, my arse. Look, when you add two and seven you get nine."

"So?"

"Well, according to the book, nine is the magic number on which all creation is built; the foundation of life itself. There are nine planets in our solar system . . ."

"There are eight."

"No, nine."

"No, eight: Earth, Mars, Mercury, Jupiter, Neptune, Saturn. How many is that? Er . . . Neptune . . ."

"You've said Neptune."

"*Venus* and . . . Uranus. That's definitely eight."

"You forgot Pluto."

"Pluto doesn't count. It's a dwarf planet."

"Dwarves *do* count."

"Not when they're planets. Or not when they're *not* planets . . ."

Throwing the book to the floor, Tony jabbed a squat finger at a poster on the wall. "*He* knew."

Beth recognised the long-nosed, bespectacled face beaming down at her. "John Lennon? He wasn't an astronomer."

"No," said Tony, "but he knew about the number nine."

"Why? Because he did a song called 'No. 9 Dream'?"

"Oh, it's *much* more than that. He was born on the 9th October. The ninth day of the ninth month."

"October is the tenth month."

"That may be so, but there are nine letters in his name . . ."

"There are 10 letters in his name."

"Well . . . he did a song called 'One After 909' . . . and 'Revolution 9'. So, you see, the number nine was important to him. And he is immortal."

"He's dead."

"Well, yes, but . . ."

"Look," Beth got up and started browsing the racks. "The dead aren't coming back to life just because you've overpriced a load of old Elvis Presley records."

"You have a better explanation?"

She examined a copy of David Bowie's *Hunky Dory*. "The crazy old man seemed to think it was a natural thing . . ."

"Who is this crazy old man you keep banging on about?"

Beth put the record down. "He kidnapped me and took me to an old building in the graveyard. He tied me up and . . ."

"There's no building in the graveyard . . ."

"There isn't any more . . ."

"It fell down, did it?"

"Yes. Marv helped me escape. Or was it his ghost?"

"Sounds barmy to me."

"Says the man who thinks the number nine can bring back the dead!"

"Well, something has, hasn't it?"

Just then, their argument was silenced by an almighty roar from outside.

44. SMASH

The torch-bearing mob were scratching at the window.

"I was wondering when they'd catch up," said Tony.

There were more of them now. Others had been gathered on the way. Doors had been knocked upon; folk had been roused from dreams.

"Grab a stick, Mavis—there's trouble."

They all gladly lit their sticks and joined the march. Those without sticks held rakes. They rapped them against the window, whilst screaming with muffled voices:

"We're gonna kill ya!"

There were about 60 or 70 of them out there in the street. Beth spied Benny at the front.

"Reverse the curse, you slag!" he spat, his scowling features pressing the glass. To think, she had once thought him kind. He looked and sounded alien now.

Then she spotted two more familiar faces in the crowd.

"Mum! Dad!"

"You're no daughter of mine," her father cried.

"I always knew you were a witch," snarled Mother.

Beth lowered her head as the mob continued to shout: "Burn 'em! Kill 'em!"

They hammered at the window until it cracked.

Smash.

A brick burst through in a spray of glass. It was followed by a blazing torch. And then another.

Tony and Beth huddled together in the centre of the shop. The torches landed on a pile of books. Tony shook his head as the pages curled and smouldered.

Suddenly, the flames lapped higher; bright orange tongues licked the Grotto walls.

"Burn 'em!"

A mass of twisted faces poked through the smashed window, shaking rakes and flinging torches.

Beth had never heard human beings make such a noise before.

"Kill 'em!"

They began to slither into the shop, their rakes and torches held high. Grins sliced their glowing faces; glass crunched under hands and feet. Some set fire to each other in excitement.

Tony didn't know what to do. His Grotto was ablaze. His little vinyl babies were burning. Black melted plastic dripped down the flaming racks. The idols on the posters all went up in smoke.

Tony ran towards the wall, flapping his arms; but he knew he couldn't put it out. He stood, numb and stooped; flames reflected in his watery eyes.

Beth couldn't see anything through the billowing black smog. Gusts of smoke poured into her nostrils, stinging her lungs and throat.

"Tony," she coughed. "Where are you?"

There was no reply.

Dark, creeping figures writhed at her feet. They grabbed her legs with burnt, peeling fingers and dragged her into the flames.

45. SMOKE

"Hold on, Beth." It was Tony's voice.

He was lost behind a wall of fire, calling through the flames. Molten vinyl oozed down the walls, dripping on his skin.

Beth heard him scream. Coughing and spluttering, she kicked and stomped at grasping hands, feeling them crack beneath her heels.

"I'm coming."

Through stinging eyes, she saw Tony emerge from the haze. His body was encased, from head to foot, in melted vinyl. Resembling some strange, black-clad mutant, he strode through the fire and lifted Beth into his shining arms.

"Come on, love," he said.

She gripped his hot plastic body as he charged through the burning crowd. Within the sizzling inferno, Beth noticed Mr Thompson, howling and flailing, whilst Janice, the café owner, batted at her smouldering limbs. Then Beth saw two charcoaled lumps, holding each other on the floor. They looked just like her parents. Burying her head against Tony's chest, she clenched her sore, damp eyes.

A thickening smog obscured Tony's vision. Flames hissed by his ears. Beth's body seemed heavier, a dead weight in his tired arms. A fresh curtain of fire roared before him. There was no way out.

Shadows glimmered through the seething mist. Tony blinked. Over to his right, he glimpsed two figures, hand in hand. It was Marv and his mother,

Victoria. The flames parted around them, as if cringing in fear.

With her free hand, Victoria clutched the old magic book to her bloodied breast, whilst Marv stared at Tony with spaniel eyes.

Shuddering, the record seller drifted towards them. Thick black smoke welled up on every side. Drawing nearer to the figures, Tony looked around. The flames were now behind him, but mother and son had vanished. Beth was still in his arms, though her breathing was as laboured as his own, and her eyes remained closed. Spinning forward, he saw the smashed shop window.

Hugging Beth to his chest, Tony clambered through the opening. Jagged shards of glass pricked his legs as he slid to the street. Remaining on his feet, he sucked in great gusts of oxygen from the smoke-filled night. Although a cool, soothing wind touched his face, he still felt insufferable heat throughout his body. Stepping away from the inferno, he began to cross the road, with Beth dangling from his arms, limp and fading.

Boom.

A belch of flame rose behind them, sending an explosion of bricks and roasted guts into the air.

Tony fell to the cold, wet pavement opposite. Rolling through puddles, he gasped and squirmed.

Beth lay sprawled beside him, her limbs at odd angles. Crawling over to check her pulse, Tony spluttered "Are you all right?", before falling back down. The crackle of fire filled his ears. Lifting his head, he observed the burning shop.

A life of dreams ablaze.

Turning away, he saw Marv and his mother at the end of the street, watching the fire spread to adjacent buildings. They were joined by an old man, grasping a crumpled paper bag. From it, he scoffed candies that fell through a slit in his throat.

Behind them, more phantoms lurched into view, including an unmistakable, headless form. It was Jonas Koop.

Tony lay back, beaming.

As flames stabbed the darkness overhead, the face of his own dead mother gazed down through swirling mists. For the first time in years, she, too, was smiling.

Tony closed his eyes. He hoped there was music, wherever he was going.

46. BLAZE

"Tony?"

Beth staggered to her feet, coughing. Brushing small, sharp stones from her knees, she squinted at the prone record seller. His chest, smothered in melted black vinyl, no longer rose or fell.

"Wake up," she croaked.

Glancing over the road, she saw the whole street was on fire now. Directly opposite, a black shape hobbled through the flames towards her.

Suddenly, it ran, screaming, from the blaze.

"Please wake up, Tony."

The black, brittle figure drew closer, its limbs like charred matchsticks, its face a bubbling mess. Flames dripped from the blackened husk; a raw, pink hole opened below two eyes glowing with hate.

"Beth. You bitch."

The voice was scratchy, but Beth recognised it—along with the scraps of flaming tracksuit which hung from the shrivelled frame.

"Benny?"

He stopped right in front of her, grimacing. His strong white teeth were still intact—as was his nose, which stuck out through knots of crisp flesh.

"You bitch," he rasped, slapping clawed hands to her throat.

The rough, blistered fingers scorched her skin—and stifled her scant, remaining breaths.

47. HEAD

Beth choked. With Tony dead, no one could save her now.

Suddenly, something came hurtling from the burning Grotto. It sailed through the air, hitting Benny on the head. Dropping his hands from Beth's neck, he staggered back, dazed. The object that struck him hovered in front of his face.

Catching her breath, Beth noted that it was a floating grey skull, whose empty black sockets gazed into Benny's wide eyes. It seemed to be grinning at him.

"Get away from me," Benny screamed.

The skull continued to grin. Then its jaw creaked open—and its rotten teeth clamped over Benny's nose.

"Get off!"

Benny shrieked as the skull bit down. It tore the nose right off his face, pulling it away in tough, gooey strands.

Falling to his knees, Benny's husk-like body crumbled in a cloud of black flakes, showering the tarmac with ash.

The skull glided over to Beth. Holding onto her nose, she shifted from foot to foot, as it hung in the flame-lit darkness before her.

Then it whizzed away along the street. Beth watched in awe as a headless, leather-jacketed shape stepped forth to claim it. When placed back upon its raw, bloody neck stump, the skull seemed to smile once more. Then all was obscured by thick fogs of smoke.

Was that Jonas Koop?

It was Beth's last thought before fainting.

48. SUNDAY

When Beth awoke again, the town was blackened ash. The fires had been extinguished by the rain, which now fell with reassuring monotony.

It was the early hours of Sunday morning. To Beth, Sundays always had a clammy feel to them, a depressing emptiness, and today was no different.

No. Today *was* different.

At her feet, Tony lay sprawled and dead, covered in vinyl and flies. The stench of burnt flesh was overpowering and atrocious. She had to get away.

Pulling her parka up over her nose, she began a dazed walk through the seared streets.

All was still and quiet. Shreds of mist seemed to erode the wasted landscape. Spirals of smoke curled into the ashen clouds.

She was relieved to see the river still rolling by. But, otherwise, nothing was left: The houses and shops were reduced to cinders; charred bodies littered the ground, their once-familiar faces a frazzled mass; and frail remnants of trees reached for each other, as if on the verge of some failed embrace.

Beneath the grey, bird-less sky, Beth glimpsed shadows on the horizon: Marv, Jonas and Tony kicked their way through mounds of powdered debris. Victoria Jeffreys beckoned alongside them.

They led Beth to the old dirt road. It lay out before her, an unspoken promise.

Those who have nothing, have nothing to lose.

She couldn't remember where she'd heard that before. But, summoned by the dead, she moved beyond the rain and took her first steps on the road that went on forever, to see if it really did.

ABOUT THE AUTHOR

A lifelong lover of movies and monsters, **Stephen Mosley**
played the monster in the movie *Kenneth*. His other acting
credits include the eponymous paranormal investigator
of *Kestrel Investigates*; the shady farmer, James, in
Contradiction; a zombie in *Zomblogalypse*; and a blink-and-
you'll-miss-it appearance opposite Sam Neill in *Peaky
Blinders*.

As well as being the author of *Klawseye: The
Imagination Snatcher of Phantom Island*, *The Lives & Deaths
of Morbius Mozella*, *The Boy Who Loved Simone Simon*, and
Christopher Lee: The Loneliness of Evil (from Midnight
Marquee Press), Stephen is one half of the music duo
Collinson Twin and has contributed to the books *Masters
of Terror*; *Mistresses of the Macabre*; *Dead or Alive: British
Horror Films 1980-1989*; *70s Monster Memories*; *Unsung
Horrors*; *A Celebration of Peter Cushing*; and *Son of Unsung
Horrors*.

His articles have appeared in magazines *Midnight
Marquee*, *We Belong Dead*, *Multitude of Movies*, and *The
Dark Side*, while his short stories have been included in
such anthologies as *Dracula's Midnight Snacks* and *Zombie
Bites*.

Please visit: www.stephenmosley.net

KLAWSEYE: THE IMAGINATION SNATCHER OF
PHANTOM ISLAND

"This book is now one of my favourites . . . It is really adventurous . . . so tense and exciting. I bet the Queen would enjoy it!"—Amelia (aged 9)

"Although this may present as a book for children, as an adult I found it thoroughly enjoyable and a welcome escape from daily life. I was engaged throughout, the author's writing style draws you in and holds your interest, it's a hard book to put down! I found the final paragraph very moving."—Mr P.G. Best

"You'd have to be a real snot-filled poo head not to enjoy this."—Kindle Customer

THE LIVES & DEATHS OF MORBIUS MOZELLA

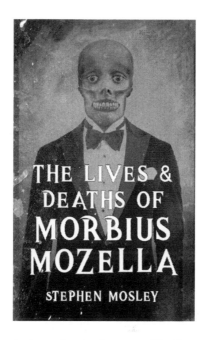

"Presents a whole orchestral score of feeling—not only the dark notes of pain, loss, unrequited love and the temptations to suicide, but also of joy and faith. In addition, it demonstrates humour of a deeply personal, gnarled, kind . . . The perfectly pitched tone and diamond hard imagery expresses contradictory feelings in prose as pure and clear as a mountain stream.

Imagine a collection of prose poems written by Vincent Price and Barbara Windsor with occasional interventions by Peter Ackroyd and Spike Milligan."—David Lancaster.

Printed in Great Britain
by Amazon

66149500R00084